HOW FAR THE
MOUNTAIN

Other Sunstone Press novels by Robert K. Swisher Jr.

The Land
Fatal Destiny
Only Magic
Love Lies Bleeding
The Last Narrow Gauge Train Robbery
The Last Day In Paradise
Touch Me If You Love Me—Poetry

Also by Robert K. Swisher Jr.

The Man From The Mountain
American Love Story
The Weaver
The Captain
Ned

HOW FAR THE MOUNTAIN

A Novel

Robert K. Swisher Jr.

SUNSTONE
PRESS

SANTA FE

Cover photograph by Leigh Smith
Book and Cover design by Vicki Ahl

Sunstone books may be purchased for educational, business, or sales promotional use. For information please write: Special Markets Department, Sunstone Press, P.O. Box 2321, Santa Fe, New Mexico 87504-2321.

Library of Congress Cataloging-in-Publication Data

Swisher, Robert K., 1947-
How far the mountain : a novel / by Robert K. Swisher Jr.
    p. cm.
  ISBN 978-0-86534-522-5 (pbk. : alk. paper)
  I. Title.

PS3569.W574H69 2007
813'.54--dc22

                                      2007001791

Published in

WWW.SUNSTONEPRESS.COM
SUNSTONE PRESS / POST OFFICE BOX 2321 / SANTA FE, NM 87504-2321 /USA
(505) 988-4418 / ORDERS ONLY (800) 243-5644 / FAX (505) 988-1025

For Deidra and Daphne

Always in my heart

The Man
A Return To Memory

Gazing out the kitchen window, the scorching cinder in the center of Bill's heart pulsed back to life. He had defeated the flame, but he could not rid himself of the smoldering embers that over the last year had charred away almost all of his feelings. "I have to touch the bones," he muttered, the flame stirring. "I must, if only for myself."

Bill could see his reflection in the dirty glass—forty six years old, a cracked and lined tough face, with a strong square jaw and a black handle bar moustache so big people could not tell if he was smiling or frowning. His gray eyes, once sparkling, were now distant, like they would rather not see. He was not tall, six feet with his boots on, big in the chest, strong shoulders with a slight gut, but he was in good shape and kept his weight at one hundred and seventy five. Even with his last two years of idleness his hands were still calloused with large swollen knuckles and fingers. His black hair, crew cut, was beginning to show white. He wore faded Levi's, held up by a leather belt, with a silver buckle from his rodeo days, a white western shirt with snaps, and he tucked his pant legs into tall, brown, leather cowboy boots with riding heels.

Bill looked through his reflection into the backyard. Two young robins were beneath the apple tree, reminding him of miniature clowns, but he did not smile. The mother robin, acting as if she did not see her children, was standing as still as a statue while her eyes waited patiently for the scurrying of a bug, or the slithering of an earthworm through the jungle of grass. The mother, suddenly tigress, taking three purposeful bounds stabbed an earthworm with her rapier beak. Bill imagined the terror filled cries of the worm as it writhed with all its might to try to escape and regain the safety of the warm, dark earth. The two young robins, alerted by their mother's quick movements, and seeing the worm thrashing from her beak, darted at her with pleading, gaping mouths. Their mother gobbled down the worm and gazed disdainfully over the heads of her astonished youngsters before resuming her solitary hunt. The two young robins chirped pitifully in their bewilderment. "You will learn," Bill said to the baby robins, who were now chasing frantically after their mother.

"After a few days of going hungry, you will learn. And after you have learned, you will forget your teacher," Bill said, as though his words would comfort the two young robins.

Stepping back from the window Bill tried to ignore the cinder in his heart. "I am tired and weary. I must go back. I must go back to the mountain," he said, as if his words were pleas.

"I must touch the bones," he added with little conviction.

After two attempts, one of the young robins captured a pale purple beetle. The other youngster rushed greedily to try and steal the doomed bug. Seeing the determined dash of his now rival, the young robin gulped down the beetle. The mother robin observed the conquest, and the victory, and the cornerstone of self, and with neither love nor remorse flew away. The two young robins did not see her go—they went off in different directions, both eyeing the ground in search of their own survival.

Bill poured himself a cup of coffee. Sipping the coffee, he closed the kitchen curtain, shutting out all but one sliver of light that sliced through the room, exposing in its radiance millions of dust particles.

Sitting in a wooden chair he placed his cup on a square wooden table that was covered with scars from years of cups and plates. A thin beam of sunshine hit Bill on the forehead. He raised his head until the ray bore directly in his eyes. His vision melted into the light and the small swirling worlds of dust. "Yes," he said forcefully, feeling the heat from the cinder in his heart. "I will go to the mountain. I will go to the mountain and I will touch the bones."

Shutting his eyes, a vision of the mountain swirled in the red spots on the back of his eyelids, and he was afraid.

The Woman
The Cemetery

"Happy Birthday," Sheila said to herself as she got out of bed, not really happy but strangely content.

"Another year older, girl," she said to her reflection in the full-length mirror attached to the front of her bedroom door. Slipping out of the pink, knee length, imitation silk nightgown she tossed it on the bed. "Not too bad for forty-two," she said, examining her naked body.

Sheila made a cheesecake pose, put her right hand behind her head, bent her knees slightly, and opened her mouth like a centerfold. The open mouth bit had always made her laugh. Straightening up, she turned sideways and tilted her head to get a better view of her profile. She had a fine, well-proportioned athletic body and an impish face that made people feel like they could talk to her. She wore her auburn hair short, but long enough to bounce when she walked. She knew men glanced at her a lot. She was not model-beautiful but she was sexy and bubbly like a young schoolteacher.

"I need a man like I need cellulite," she laughed to her reflection.

She tried to laugh as much as possible, it seemed to help, and it kept her sadness partially at bay.

Leaning closer to the mirror she scrutinized the tiny crow's feet in the corners of her soft green eyes. "Experience," she said, making a haughty face and pushing his touch from her mind.

Dressing, she put on a pair of loose fitting faded Levi's, a gray sweatshirt and tennis shoes. By noon she had finished her normal Saturday routine. The house was clean. The plants hanging in every window were watered and all the dead leaves picked off. The washing machine was churning away with all her respectable work clothes as she called them, those that did not have to go to the dry cleaners. At one time she wished she could have worn Levi's or sweats to sell real estate, but she had gotten over it after her first big sale. Now, with her own company, she wore her business suits and matching outfits as more of her personal joke on the world. "Hell," she told herself one day, "nobody has to know I'm an old hippie at heart."

Now, nobody really knew what or who she was. He had known her as much as another person possibly could. She tried to tell herself it really did not matter, but she knew it was a lie, wanting desperately for someone to know her and share with her.

After the dryer was going, she brushed her hair, drank two glasses of orange juice and left the house. It was a beautiful day. Several neighbors were mowing their yards. She did not wave to them as she drove by in her new light blue Chevy four door.

Entering the cemetery she tried not to be depressed. She always liked cemeteries, but that was before his death. As a young girl she and her aunt would go to cemeteries and read the headstones. There was something peaceful and timeless in a cemetery then. Everything was in order. Everything neat and tidy like a little boy sitting in church with his hair slicked down and his shoes shined.

Driving slowly through the older part of the cemetery the headstones had a fearless and brave dignity that embraced death—the huge cottonwoods and oaks spreading like wise and ancient prophets over the headstones.

The newer stones were like all the newer houses she sold, too plain, too identical, too conforming, too everything. "We are all individuals of sameness," she thought, without being bitter or sad.

The trees in the newer part of the cemetery were infants. Anywhere else Sheila would have liked the young trees. But, here they bothered her. Death was not new, was not an infant. Death deserved shade and majesty.

Parking the car, Sheila turned off the ignition and sat for several moments staring at a hill of dirt from a freshly dug grave. Two starlings perched on the top of the pile of dirt. For an instant she imagined a crying widow standing by the coffin. "No," she commanded herself. "No."

Going to the grave a man and woman were praying solemnly at another headstone while, not far away, a young boy and girl played.

By the grave Sheila forced a small smile over her thin lips. "I still have a great body, good legs, flat stomach, and my boobs don't sag," she said to the grave.

A slight breeze kicked, carrying the sound of children's laughter like the tinkle of far away silver bells to her ears. She sat down next to the grave as if by sitting she would be closer to what had been. "You know I only come here on my birthday," she said distantly.

She did not see the man and the woman glance over at her.

"It's been two years and I'm still not in love. Can you imagine?"

Her bravery began cracking like the delicate milky porcelain on an antique doll.

The man called to the children who ran to him. Putting his hand on the boy's head he said, "You must be quiet, there's a lady over there and we don't want to disturb her."

The two children did not say anything to each other.

"I've met lots of men," Sheila continued. "It's not that I wouldn't like to be in love. I would. You know that. But I haven't met anybody who wants me. They all want something that isn't me," she said, weighing her words carefully. "They want me because of my job. Or the way I dress. Or my smile. Or my eyes. My hair." She forced a giggle. "Okay, okay, my body. But, at my age it's either the young ones who need a mother, or the old ones who need a bauble. My luck, huh?"

She noticed the man and woman and the two children walking toward a white minivan. She wanted to wave, but it did not seem quite right. "I'd like to be in love," she said to the headstone. "Or maybe I'd like somebody to love me. I don't think I would have to love them if they loved me. Really loved me."

Picking a blade of grass that was taller than the others she twirled it between her fingers. "I'd even like a good male friend. Somebody I could go dancing with, or out to eat, somebody with no demands. Don't laugh, I know—a man with no demands. That's a joke."

Standing, she brushed the grass from her pants. "We were good for each other. I want you to know that," she said. "And I want you to know I'm fine. I can take care of myself. You always said I was strong and independent and could take care of myself. You were right."

For a brief moment she could see his face as he was dying and the tubes, like veins, running into his deflated body. "You are strong, I love you," he said, through the drug haze and the pain.

The family in the minivan drove away. "Poor lady," the woman said to her husband. "She is probably alone."

"Will you get us an ice cream?" the young girl asked her father.

Sheila started toward her car but stopped and went back to the grave. "I forgot to tell you," she said. "I'm going backpacking up in the mountains by myself. It's my birthday present to me. I'm taking a week off and going up to the mountains. Doesn't it sound grand and brave?"

After a few moments she went to her car, noticing for the first time the chorus of singing birds that filled the air. In the car she saw two men begin pitching a tent by the freshly dug grave. Starting the car, she thought, "I loved him but now he is only a memory, a warm memory, no different than a joyful dream, or a pressed flower in a book."

But, she knew he was more than a memory.

Driving back to the house she was making a mental list of what she must buy for her backpacking trip to the mountains and pondering where she wanted to go. She was excited about her adventure. Not happy, but strangely content and trying to be brave.

The Mountain
Before Time Remembers

The mountain is not a special mountain even though it is the caretaker of the bones. It is not one of those majestic mountains that people speak of with awe in their voices. When it comes to mountains the mountain is like a small unassuming town that people speed through on their way to the big city lights of Chicago, New York, San Francisco or Denver. The small towns that people only stop in when the car needs gas, or they need a quick bite to eat, or a child has to go to the bathroom.

The mountain is only a hill compared to the other mountains that loom around it. The other mountains have imposing granite snow capped peaks with haloes of clouds circling them like wise old men's beards—the old men peer down on the mountain like it is only a gangly teenager in the company of worldly adults.

The mountain is also a nuisance to those journeying to more dramatic mountains. A temporary distraction they must navigate to reach parts of nature worthy of an adventurous human being's time.

But still, it is a mountain. A beautiful mountain in its own right, even though its top does not rest with the clouds—a mountain that has been a salt water ocean bottom, the shore of a fresh water sea, and bubbling rivers of molten rock. It has been the resting place for a great scouring glacier that reduced it to level land. But it tenaciously pushed itself up from the rubble to once again become a mountain. The mountain has been home to clams the size of truck tires, sharks as large as modern whales, ferns that would shade the largest of houses, fish beyond imagination and dinosaurs from the size of rabbits to four-story houses. Now, it is home to deer, elk, beaver, grouse, blue jays, bears, pine, spruce, and cedar trees, with a few scattered clumps of aspens on its sides as if a lonely giant tossed them there only for his pleasure.

It is a mountain that, although mostly ignored, a few have journeyed to—people content with the simple things in life, satisfied to sit on its sides and say, "This is a nice mountain. I like it, it suits me."

When it comes to mountains, it is only a hill that on a National Geographic Survey Map states its top is 8,182 feet. Looking at the map a person can see the dotted trails that meander along its sides and lead to the other postcard perfect mountains, the ones people climb to try and talk to God, as if God really wants to listen.

The old-timers, living in a small town in the valley, do not have a name for the mountain. It is simply a bump that somehow got mixed up with all those real mountains.

But, even being insignificant, it too has been plundered in its time. Its sides were stripped of its huge pine and blue spruce trees—trees that were so large three men could not stretch their arms around the massive trunks. But the forest has grown back among the huge stumps that lay rotting on the ground like the remains of gigantic hippos—young trees reaching for the stars even though they are only a few feet around—if left alone these trees could also bring wonder to the minds of men with their size and tenacity, and maybe, a few of those minds will realize how small we of the human race really are—how small and fleeting.

The mountain has been fortunate that gold or silver was never found in quantity in its veins of quartz, or uranium in its silted rock underbelly. Many dug and blasted but the mountain was barren in the eyes of the fortune seekers—as if not having enough gold or silver is an embarrassment.

And through it all—the salt water ocean, the fresh water sea, the glaciers, the molten rock, the creatures as big and powerful as tanks, and the fortune seekers—the mountain has endured.

If it is true what many wish to believe, that the earth does not live, does not breathe, and sustain, or nurture—that the earth is nothing but rock and water, here for our will to dig and probe and cut and smash, then the mountain does not care, or feel, or hope, or dream.

It is only a small mountain, a random shape made from silt and volcanoes and the slipping and sliding of the earth's crust. It is only time—endless, senseless, enduring time.

But, to some, it is more than a hill, more than a circle on a National Geographic Survey Map, it is a living breathing world. A world with a soul and a heart, even though at times its heart is black and uncaring.

In the world of mountains it is not much of a mountain, but to a man and a woman, unknowing to each other, it will be a climb to both heaven and hell and a source of redemption.

The Man
<u>To Touch The Bones</u>

Bill Johnson was by the gate to the corral. Weeds now grew where once ten horses had galloped and whinnied when he approached. Opening the gate Bill ambled to the water tank, making a disgusted face. The tank was half full of green, stagnant water. In the murky water, thousands of mosquito larvae wiggled in their evil birth dance. With little effort he pushed the tank over on its side and found great satisfaction in knowing the mosquitoes would all die. He hated mosquitoes. He hated mosquitoes even worse than flies. God must have been feeling ornery when he created mosquitoes and flies.

Bill went to a red, tin, horse barn and brought back a hose from one of the dusty stalls. Connecting the hose to the outside spigot he washed out the inside of the water tank. Finished, he curled the hose over a post and leaned back against the corral. He looked disdainfully at the barn—at the water tank—at the house. She had loved it all, ten acres of heaven she called it. After working and saving for years they bought the ten acre lot, built a nice two bedroom house, the corral, added the tin barn with horse stalls, fenced it all, and settled in. They had enough money and invested wisely and though they were not rich, they were comfortable, and he had his guiding business. After all the years they could ride their horses, she could paint, and he could hunt and fish whenever he liked. "Ten acres of heaven," Bill muttered. "Ten acres of hell. What is the difference between Heaven and Hell?"

Taking a deep breath Bill gazed at the gently rolling land. The pinion and cedar trees melted into the deep browns and grays of the rock and earth like they were all one. It was beautiful. From the lot not another house was visible. On the horizon were the dark outlines of the Rocky Mountains—distant uncaring ghosts. He forced himself to look at the peaks. He forced himself to think about the bones.

A female German Shepherd with a graying muzzle ran over to the corral and sat by Bill's foot. Bill scratched behind her ears. "Gypsy, you old worthless dog, where in the hell have you been?"

Thumping her tail a few times on the ground the dog lay down, seemingly at rest with the world. Bill remembered when Gypsy wandered into his life. Waking early one cold winter morning the German Shepherd was sitting on the front porch like she belonged there. He fed her, at which she showed no great thanks, and then she followed him around while he fed the horses and broke the ice on the water tank. When he went back in the house the dog lay down on the porch. "There's a good looking dog on the porch," he told her during breakfast.

All she said was, "Get rid of it, I don't like dogs."

That had been over ten years ago. "She loved you," Bill said to the dog. "As much as I loved her."

Gypsy thumped her bushy tail several times but did not get up. Love had no great impact on her life.

Bill stretched—the warm June air feeling good on his face. He was raised on a large cattle ranch, which the family lost. He rode broncos at local rodeos for years, never quite good enough to go to the finals, but still good enough to pick up some pocket change at the state level. After he was too old to rodeo, he sold horses; racehorses, meat horses, kid's horses, it did not matter, he sold them all. Then he guided for many years.

He guided high mountain horseback hunting trips, fishing trips, and photography trips—guided all the city slickers, as he called them, took them up to the mountains so they could eat candy bars and granola and see the real world. "The real world," he half cursed, thinking about the wall tents with wood stoves in them, and the cots with air mattresses on them. The meals included steak dinners and breakfasts with eggs and pancakes. He laughed sarcastically thinking abut the fancy dans hanging onto the horses like kids hanging onto the toy horses their mothers put them on in front of K-Marts and Wal-Marts.

He half smiled. It had been fun though, it made him feel good about what he was—a cowboy. "Cowboy my ass," he smirked to Gypsy, making the dog jump to her feet. "I never could stand John Wayne, how can I be a cowboy?"

Bill headed toward the barn, the dog, as usual, ten feet in front of him, as if she knew his every thought and action. Gypsy's tail stuck straight up in the air. Unlike most German Shepherds, her tail did not curve, but stuck up in the air like the tail of a deer bolting away in fright.

The inside of the barn was dark and dusty. Bill opened all the stall doors and both the front and back doors, letting the warm sunshine wash into the barn. Bill went into a small room and turned on the light. On the walls hung lead ropes, halters, bits from snaffles to hackamores, tie downs, and several hemp lariats. On saddle stands were three saddles and two packsaddles. Up against the wall was a set of wooden panniers, the ends bent from hitting trees. On a table were canvas tarps all folded and stacked neatly that were used to cover the panniers. At one time Bill owned enough gear to outfit six packhorses and haul in four people. On top of a stove for a wall tent was an eight-foot by twelve-foot tent that was handmade in Oregon from white sailcloth. When it was pitched, with its pine poles and lashings, and the stovepipe sticking out the flew hole, it made a mountain meadow into a home. Gypsy whined several times. "You loved it too," he said to the dog.

Gypsy jumped up in the air, shaking her head. "Yea, we will go," Bill said. "I wouldn't leave you behind, never could leave you behind."

The dog sniffed the tent, pulling out of the fabric the odors of bacon, steaks, fried trout, and the blood of deer and elk.

Bill noticed his spurs hanging from a saddle horn as he went out of the room. The dog did not follow, but stood eyeing him. "Get out of there," he ordered the dog. "I told you we would go."

The dog ran by his leg and raced out the front door of the barn, running around the barn several times before she stopped once more by his leg. Bill laughed, a shallow laugh, but still a laugh, and reaching down he patted the dog on her heaving side. "You're not worth the dog food I feed you," he said.

The dog's tail thumped on the ground.

Bill inspected a green, dented and battered, two-horse trailer, surprised the tires were still inflated. The dog whined, looking at him with her smoky topaz eyes. "I told you already," he said to the dog. "We will go, don't bother me again about it."

Heading toward the house the dog ran in front of him. When he went inside she sat down on the porch like she always did, not looking at the door but out at the trees and the land, as if the ten acres went on forever, as if it was a real ranch, and not what the realtors called a ranchette. When Bill brought out her food she did not jump up and down. She waited calmly until he set down the dish, and, only after he went back inside, did she eat.

Sitting at the kitchen table Bill stared at the distant mountain. His heart started pounding in his chest and sweat popped out on his forehead. "You can kill me if you want," he said grimly, "but I'm coming, I'm coming."

As his heart slowed down, Gypsy strolled into the backyard. She barked at two robins, which flew into a tree, and then she lay down in the sun.

Bill smiled. "You're a good dog," he said looking at the old graying German Shepherd, "you're a good old worthless dog."

When Bill came out of the house with a can of saddle soap to clean up his tack, the dog beat him to the barn. When he started rubbing the soap into the first saddle, she lay down on the floor and shut her eyes. "You remember too," Bill said to the dog. "You remember, you're just stronger than I am."

Late in the afternoon Bill opened the door to his pickup truck. No sooner was the door open then Gypsy was in the truck and sitting by the other window.

Gary Lindsey, foreman of the 150,000 acre Stone Ranch, saw the approaching truck, and spit a gob of tobacco. He had three horses to shoe and he did not really have time to talk. But, when he recognized the truck, he was sad.

Gary approached the truck, trying to hide the pain in his back. Bill got out and Gypsy darted by him. Gary held out his hand to shake. "Haven't seen you in a long time," he said, looking deeply into Bill's eyes. He then glanced at the dog. "You want to sell that dog yet?"

"No," Bill replied simply.

Gypsy ignored them as though she knew she was being talked about.

"Going to be able to hang on?" Bill asked.

"Who in the hell knows? Boss is trying to do some deal with the state so we can give them land and not have to pay taxes for a few years. Maybe, maybe not."

"I need two horses," Bill told Gary. "Two mountain horses."

"Buy or borrow?" Gary asked.

"Borrow."

Gary spit a gob of tobacco. "It's about time you went back Bill," he said, in only a manner an old and trusted friend could.

"I know," Bill replied.

"You could get you another string and start guiding again," Gary said.

"How's the wife?" Bill asked, ignoring the statement.

"Not as good of company as that dog," Gary smiled. "Kid is Rodeo Queen this year."

"She always was good with horses."

"All I got to do now is keep her from getting knocked up by some dumb rodeo cowboy."

"Good luck," Bill said, smiling.

Gary nodded toward a large corral. "I got two horses over here a green horn like you can handle. One packs good, a little stubborn, but easy to handle, not mean," Gary said.

"I'll pick them up in a few days," Bill said.

"That's okay, I'll bring them over tomorrow," replied Gary. "I have to go into town and get some truck parts."

Bill opened the door to the truck, Gypsy jumped in. "Sure you don't want to sell that dog?" Gary asked.

Bill shook his head as he shut the door.

"I'm glad you're going back," Gary said, reaching into the truck and putting his hand on Bill's shoulder.

"Thanks," Bill said.

"You take care of this worthless old cowboy," Gary said to Gypsy.

Gypsy laid her ears back and growled at Gary. "That's a damn good dog," Gary said. "A damn good dog."

After Bill got home, he sat out on the back porch. Gypsy chased away the robins and went to lie down by the tree. Bill glared at the distant mountains. "I hate you," he said. "I hate you."

The Woman
Pocahontas

Sheila Abrams was sitting cross-legged and barefoot in the middle of her living room floor. She had on a pair of red cotton short pants and a loose fitting T-shirt that read, "I'd rather have a dog than a man." The deep weave of the peach-colored shag carpet was like cool grass caressing her toes. The radio was turned to a classical station. Standing, she turned off the radio and examined the array of camping gear arranged neatly on the floor. Erected in the corner was a blue nylon, lightweight, two-person tent. She had taken it down and put it up over a dozen times so it was now no harder to erect than making the bed. In the tent was a roll-up sleeping mat and a goose-down sleeping bag. After sleeping on it the night before, she was mildly surprised when her back did not hurt in the morning. Next to the tent was an aluminum framed pack, also blue, with two large compartments, four smaller ones, and elastic cords with hooks on the end to attach her tent and sleeping bag. Placed around the pack, like a display in an outdoor shop, were: a folding aluminum mess kit complete with knife, spoon, and fork; a canteen; a flashlight with extra batteries; a small portable propane stove with two gas cylinders; a candle powered lamp with five spare candles for her tent; twenty packs of waterproof matches; three disposable lighters; a plastic jar of biodegradable soap which she could also use to brush her teeth; a compass; four pairs of socks; two small forest green towels; a toothbrush; a brush and comb; a bottle of bug repellent; a small medicine kit; and, three large plastic bags to haul out her garbage.

Several yards from the pack were: two pairs of brown hiking shorts with double pleats; a long pair of pants, also brown; two loose fitting short sleeved shirts; a sweater; an orange stocking cap in case a poacher would mistake her for a deer; a light weight coat; two jogging bras; three pairs of cotton underwear; and, a yellow rain suit with a hood. Sheila ran her hands through her hair and inspected the gear one more time with a discerning eye. "I don't know how the Indians made it without all this stuff," she said jokingly to herself.

Sitting on the sofa she put on two pairs of blue cotton socks, which reached to her knees before she rolled them down. She then put on a pair of tan hiking boots that she bought after being told by the clerk they did not need to be broken in. She made sure she did not lace the boots too tightly. After she bought the boots, she had listened like a young child to his first grade teacher about how she should wear two pairs of socks and to make sure she dried her socks every evening. It was also better to sleep in her sleeping bag at night with no clothes on—an idea she did not like, as she could picture herself running stark naked from a bear, only to be saved by two fishermen who would not give her any clothes and would laugh at her 'pinch-an inch.'

She went to the kitchen, wiggling her toes in the new hiking boots as if testing the word of the salesman. She examined the packets of dried food on the kitchen table as intensely as if she were an infantry soldier heading into battle. There were packets of noodles with garlic butter, rice and chicken, beef stew, pudding, dried apples, dried apricots, raisins, chicken bouillon cubes, and a box of assorted natural teas. Satisfied she had enough food, she went back to the living room and removed the boots and socks, checking the red nail polish on her toes. Putting on a pair of reading glasses she picked up the topography map of the mountain she had decided to hike. She had not really been the one to make the decision, once again, it had been the store clerk. "It's not a difficult hike," he told her. "A good one for you to do since you have never been camping before. You wouldn't want to take on a tough mountain and destroy any chances of ever going hiking again."

She thought about the young face of the clerk, a face that looked as though he had hiked every inch of the Rocky Mountains, a trusting, tanned, outdoor face. For a moment she wondered if the vivid blue eyes had duped her, but she drove the momentary fear from her mind. "I can do it," she said. "I have to do it."

She studied the map with its elevation lines and trail markings, at the small blue meandering lines of an unnamed stream. She could picture the tall pine trees and the stars. She could see herself sitting by the fire all alone with the world. Taking off her glasses she lay down on the sofa and a deep sadness rolled over her like a cold ocean wave. "I miss you so at times," she said as if she was talking to a dream. "It's like I'm alive but not alive. I've lived but I haven't lived. I never wanted to prove I was strong. You were the one who was supposed to be strong."

Shutting her eyes she drove the thoughts from her mind, feeling empty with their going, but glad they were gone. "I wonder if I'm truly alive?" she wondered. "If I'm alive and this is the real world. Life seems so unreal most of the time."

The doorbell interrupted her questions. She peered out the peephole before she opened the door. Sylvia swept past her like a vivacious tornado, long red hair bouncing, bright red lipstick, and a tight dress—the odor of the latest perfume in her wake. Sheila had a momentary vision of men barking and snarling at each other as they followed Sylvia's scent trail. Eyeing the camping gear Sylvia shook her head in bewilderment. "I can't believe it," she said. "You're going to go up to the mountains. Lord, all you are going to do is break your nails and make your hair dry out. Whatever possessed you? Why don't you take flying lessons or something sane? You've never been camping in your life."

"Why don't you come with me?" Sheila asked.

"The only way I'll go camping is in a suite in Vegas," Sylvia smiled. "I don't want to let the hair grow on my legs and smell like a dog. All the nature I need I can watch on educational TV. Pocahontas you're not," Sylvia said, feigning a mocking tone.

"Have you ever been alone?" Sheila asked. "Really alone. I don't mean lonely. I mean alone."

"I don't think about it," Sylvia said in a not so convincing tone.

"I've been alone, but it's not like being alone," Sheila continued. I've been alone in a noisy bubble. I want to go to the mountains and truly be alone for once in my life. I want to sit and look at the stars and the trees and the rocks and be alone and think—think about what my mind wants to think about and not what the world wants."

"You might break," Sylvia said seriously. "You might not like what you find."

Sheila could not stop the tear that rolled down her left cheek as if it had its own mind and mission. "I've really needed you," she said quietly. "You've been such help."

Sylvia handed a hanky to Sheila not commenting on the tear. "I don't think I could be alone even if I wanted to," she said. "I've been around people so long I really don't know who or what I am. I think I become what people want me to be. Some men want a slut, some a mother, some a toy. I've acted out all of them. I'm a secretary, a waitress, a cook, a mother, but what am I? I haven't known who I am for so long it doesn't really matter anymore."

Shrugging her shoulders, Sylvia added. "Maybe you are Pocahontas," feeling a deep sadness for her friend, but not showing it.

Sheila laughed. "You want to try out some of my camping food?"

"You mean that dried stuff that costs so much and should be fed to Marines?"

"You've got it."

"No thanks, I just came by to see how the explorer was and see if I could talk her out of her madness."

"You can't."

By the door the two women hugged. "Don't let me harp on it, but you'll break all your nails," Sylvia said with an understanding smile.

"Thanks for coming by," Sheila said.

"You're a case," Sylvia told her. "You're a case but I love you."

Sheila listened to the click of Sylvia's heels as she walked down the sidewalk. After she heard the car drive away she went to the bathroom and cut off her nails.

Back in the living room she shut the curtains and crawled into the tent. She rolled out her sleeping bag on the sleeping pad and took off all her clothes before she got into the bag. The nylon was cool on her skin but in a few moments she was warm. The warmth felt good, a deep warmth. "I'm so alone," she whispered as she zipped the sleeping bag up to her chin. "Why did you die and leave me?"

The Mountain
Where The Demons Rest

On one side of the small clearing is a thick stand of aspen trees. The green and vibrant leaves chattering like chipmunks in the June breeze. Coming out of the aspens is a seldom used trail, carpeted with last year's rotting yellow and orange leaves. On the north side of the clearing, a thick stand of pines grow, so thick the sun never reaches the pine needle covered earth. Around the pine trees, patches of snow cling to their last gasps of life. During some winters the meadow is under twenty feet of snow. After these winters, the summer sun will not completely melt the snow in the pine trees.

On the eastern side of the clearing, a spring bubbles out of the ground at the base of a car sized red rock that was left behind eons ago by a glacier that grew tired of its burden. The spring forms a clear pool no more than four feet across and six inches deep. The top of the rock is covered by droppings from gray camp robbers that sit on the rock waiting patiently for bugs to hatch from the swampy earth. In the rich wet ground by the spring, delicate pink elephant's ears sway in the breeze. In the drier soil, red and orange fire brush bloom.

A trail cuts directly through the center of the meadow and exits through a stand of virgin growth spruce, their silver edged needles glistening like frost during all seasons of the year. Here, deer hide, listening and smelling the air, before cautiously tip toeing to the spring to drink. Here, also, elk rest on their yearly migrations up and down the mountain. Occasionally a black bear skirts the meadow, never brave enough to show itself in the open. There have been too many close calls—safety is only in the dark heart of the trees.

In the middle of the meadow, not far from the trail, the bones are scattered—white, sun bleached bones, bones now devoid of any flesh or hide, showing the teeth marks of skunks and badgers and porcupines and mountain lions.

The skull rests in a clump of blue mountain iris, several yards away from the spine and leg bones. Tiny blue flowers, no larger than a baby's fingernail, bloom through the eyeholes of the skull.

The spine, leg bones, and other bones are covered by tall swaying grass. A person walking or riding through the meadow would not easily see the bones.

At times the camp robbers sit on the bones, even roll over the smaller rib bones and disjointed back vertebra to look for grubs or worms, or maggots. At one time, when the flesh still clung to them, the bones had been feasts to hawks and buzzards. Now they are merely bones; dry, white, bones—bones like old and weathered headstones in graveyards.

Not far from the bones, on the side of the meadow that catches the morning sun, and back in the trees, are cut pine poles over twelve feet long. Poles used to erect a wall tent. There is also a round grill used to place over a fire and support a heavy coffeepot. Partially covered by tall grass is a fire pit with its circle of rocks. Now, tiny white flowers, the size of ice crystals, poke their way through the charred earth. On the edge of the trees is a half rotten stack of cut and split firewood, piled up for another planned trip—a wasted effort, as though one had kidded himself and felt he could foretell the future and plan.

It is a beautiful mountain meadow. But there are the bones. The white, dry, gravestone bones.

The Man
The Beginning Of The Quest

It was slightly past midnight when Bill reached the trailhead. He had not left his house until after the sun went down, not wanting to see the mountains as he drove toward them, although he had loaded his gear in the early afternoon. Bill turned off the lights to the truck, feeling as though he was stranded in a life raft in the middle of the ocean and there was no hope he would ever be found. Gypsy whined softly and poked him with her cold nose. He patted the top of her head, enjoying the feeling of her thick hair. "I guess I have to move," he said to the dog.

Getting out of the truck, Gypsy barreled past him and dashed into the darkness. The small bell Bill had attached to her collar tinkled like a tiny wind chime. He got his flashlight out from behind the seat. When he shined the light at the trailer window, the horses neighed and stomped their feet. Taking out the first horse he put a set of hobbles on her front legs and turned her out. When he had done the same thing with the second horse, he tossed two wedges of hay by the rear of the horse trailer. The horses waited for him to leave before coming to eat.

Bill could hear the stream that was no more than fifty yards away. He liked the sound of the stream. It had been a long time. He could no longer hear the bell, but he did not worry, Gypsy would be back. He never had to worry about Gypsy, she knew what she was doing. Bill had never tied up Gypsy. He would never tie up the dog.

Taking a canvas tarp from the back of the truck he spread it on the ground and put his sleeping bag on top of the canvas. From the back of the truck he took out an arm full of wood. After stacking the wood, he sprayed it with kerosene from a plastic bottle. The fire danced to life with one match, illuminating the trees around him. For a moment it reminded him of flares, but the thought of flares no longer bothered him—the war no longer bothered him. The tall, dark, imposing trees, illuminated by the fire made him feel small. Standing by the fire he shined his flashlight on the trail marker, 'Designated Wilderness Area Beyond This Point.' "Wilderness my ass," he thought.

Wilderness to only the soft remnants of mankind that most people had become. He got larger pieces of wood from the back of the truck and put them on the fire. When they caught, he got his thermos and sat down on his sleeping bag. He noticed several burn holes in the sleeping bag he had forgotten to fix. Pouring himself a cup of black coffee Gypsy tinkled in from the dark and sat down on the end of the canvas. She was wet from the stream. Bill went to the truck and returned with several packets of moist dog food. After unwrapping them he tossed them to the dog and burnt the wrappers. She sniffed them, looked around casually, and lay down to eat. Gypsy was not a dog to show thanks.

When the fire had burned down to embers, Bill removed his boots and got into his sleeping bag. He did not take off his clothes, sleeping in the nude in the boondocks was an old wives' tale. He rolled the canvas tarp over him, making the dog move. "Go find yourself a bush," he told Gypsy.

Shutting his eyes he could hear the steady grinding of the horses jaws as they ate the hay. The stream seemed to get louder as though he was lying by the bank. For now, everything was fine. It was dark and it was fine.

He was about to fall asleep when Gypsy curled up on the bottom of the tarp. He did not kick her off, but moved his legs to give her more room.

Waking, the horizon was a light crimson. The sun would clear the mountains in less than thirty minutes. A heavy dew covered the tarp and the grass. He sat up and Gypsy stretched and yawned. The horses had not gone far during the night. He tossed out a small wedge of hay and they crow hopped over on their hobbled legs. Bill thought about an old mountain horse he once had that could travel miles at night hobbled. He wondered if the horse was still alive or had been made into dog food.

Digging out a dented and black metal coffeepot Bill filled it with water from a canteen. He put the last of his wood on the embers from the night's fire and set the pot on them and tossed a handful of coffee in the pot. By the time the coffee boiled he would have all his gear packed and ready to load on the packhorse. Gypsy scampered after a ground squirrel, which made it, chattering all the way to his hole. Gypsy dug furiously for a few seconds, stuck her nose in the hole, lifted her head back up and ran back to the truck not stupid enough to waste her time on a task she could not win. Bill unwrapped two pieces of deer jerky. One he gave to the dog and one he ate himself.

When the sun cleared the ridge of the valley Bill was drinking a cup of coffee. Steam poured off the stream and the cries of two ravens filled the cool morning. He could not see the ravens. For a moment he felt like loading all the gear back into the truck and going back home. Gypsy looked at him, jumped up and down several times like she was dancing and yipped and ran toward a walking bridge that crossed the stream. When she got to the bridge, she stopped and looked back over her shoulder. "Come on back here you worthless dog," Bill called.

Gypsy ran back to him and Bill rubbed her around the neck and head. Gypsy barked, the bark echoing up the valley. "At least they're no people around," Bill told Gypsy.

Gypsy barked once again and wagged her tail.

Bill took a deep breath, looked at the horses and then back at the dog.

Within thirty minutes Bill had the packhorse loaded with all the gear and tied down with a diamond hitch. The hitch had taken three times for him to throw—it had been a long time.

He poured the rest of the coffee on the fire and put the pot in his saddlebag. As he put his foot in the stirrup, he once again felt like leaving. Taking his foot out of the stirrup he rested his forehead on the saddle and shut his eyes. After a few minutes, with little physical effort, but great mental effort, he swung up in the saddle. He unwrapped the lead rope to the pack saddle horse from his saddle horn, nudged his horse gently and started toward the stream. Gypsy ran across the bridge but Bill led his horse through the stream. The horse did not slow up or show any alarm as she picked her way through the belly deep water, nor did the pack horse pull back on her lead rope. On the other side of the stream, both horses shook. The packhorse's load did not shift and Bill felt proud. Settling into the saddle he pointed the horse toward the trail that cut through the middle of a wide green valley, dotted with stands of pine and mountain willow. Gypsy ran to the front of the horses, not looking back.

Bill fought a deep sense of loneliness as he nudged the horse on. The horse did not walk as fast as he liked a mountain horse to walk but it really did not matter. He was in no hurry and he was not going to go far the first day, only five or six miles.

After an hour Bill found himself thinking about all his years in the mountains and it was a shock to realize what he had become over the past two years. Before her, he always had the feeling he belonged in the mountains. There was no place else he had ever belonged. It was as if he walked through life two steps out of synk with everybody else, or even two steps behind. In the mountains, he moved to his own time. "I'd just as soon been an outlaw and had to hide out in the mountains my whole life," he said to the back of the horse's head although the mountains had been crueler to him than the war.

The horse's ears moved as he talked. Gypsy darted off the trail after something Bill could not see.

Bill did not stop for lunch. When he crossed small streams he let the horses drink but he did not let them grab at tufts of grass as they walked. He hated horses that did not watch where they were going. Stupid horses he called them. Mountain horses could not be stupid horses. But then, Bill mused, whoever heard of a smart horse?

At 3 p.m., Bill stopped at the mouth of a meadow. He had climbed about 2,000 feet in elevation from the trailhead. The meadow was over a mile long and not over a hundred yards wide. It was hemmed in by towering outcroppings of rock with a stream tumbling down one side. On the other side of the meadow stands of birch dotted the steep hills, while a few scattered pine trees jutted toward the sky along the edge of the stream. There was plenty of grass for the horses. Bill's legs were growing tight after not riding for two years and a small ache was creeping into the small of his back.

After unsaddling the horses Bill hobbled them and turned them out. They immediately started to eat the green grass. He did not bother to pitch the tent but made a make shift lean-to out of a tarp.

Gypsy lay in the shade of a tree and snapped at flies while Bill went through the gear looking for a frying pan and other odds and ends. When he was done, although it would not be dark for several hours, he gathered a pile of wood.

When he sat down, Gypsy sat by his side. Resting his arm around her back he patted her head. "I can see her everywhere," he told the dog. "I can hear her laugh."

Gypsy lay and rested her chin on his leg. "You're a good old dog," Bill said. "You're a good old worthless dog."

The Woman
The Beginning Of The Search

Sheila was outside of town before the morning rush hour. It was a beautiful sunshiny day with only a few meandering clouds. She felt like a model for a women's outdoor clothing company. She was wearing khaki hiking shorts, hiking boots with cotton red socks folded barely below her knees, a white light-weight cotton shirt and a plaid over shirt with the sleeves rolled up.

Her camping gear was in the back of the car. All she had to do was put the backpack on and start walking. Since it was such a nice day, she rolled down her window and let the air whip her hair around. "If the weather will only stay like this," she thought as she turned on the radio and searched for a rock and roll station.

Finding a station, she did not like the song that was playing and turned it off. There were times she could not listen to music—it brought back a flood of memories, memories that were too difficult to push away. It would be easier if she had hated her husband. Then she could ignore the memories and feel elated with her freedom.

Driving toward the mountains she did not think about the office or anything to do with work. She glanced at a book on the dash and read the title, Wild Mountain Flowers—Trees And Edible Mushrooms. She pictured the golden chanterelle mushroom that grew in the Rockies. It had amazed her when she found out that the chanterelle mushrooms went for over twenty five dollars a pound in town. She hoped to find some. Some people went to the mountains to kill elk and deer, not feeling satisfied if they did not, she was on a mushroom quest. She grinned, "Sheila, woman mushroom slayer of North America."

The road climbed into the mountains and Sheila relaxed, as if she had traveled a great distance and everything was new: new sights, new sounds, new people—nothing to remind her of the past, only the future.

As she turned off the blacktop and onto the rutted gravel road that would lead her to where she would start her hike, she had a momentary pang of apprehension. "Lord," she said. "Some women run dog sleds across Alaska alone. I can spend a week by myself."

The road ran beside a small stream littered with old tires, pop and beer cans and various other marks of civilization. The scattered forest signs were riddled with bullet holes. She visualized in her mind, men dressed in camouflage clothing with shaggy beards, standing by a battered pickup truck. The back of the truck was full of empty beer cans and they were shooting signs with rifles big enough to kill elephants. With each new hole the men would laugh. "Takes a real intelligent person to get his jollies shooting holes in signs," Sheila said as she drove by a sign she could not read because of all the bullet holes.

Luckily, the sign that had the number of the trail she wanted had only a few bullet holes in it and she turned and drove to the back of a well maintained camping area with picnic tables and barbecue pits. She was glad nobody was camping. None of the trees around the area had lower limbs, or any that could be reached unless with a ladder. They had all been chopped off and burnt by hordes of weekend campers. She read a sign, 'Sterling Peak, 23 miles'. The meadow she had picked to hike to was only seventeen miles, but, for a moment, it seemed like thousands of miles.

Getting out of the car the wind blowing through the trees was the only sound she heard. It was strange and eerie, almost alien, after hearing the sound of the city for so long.

At first the wind hitting the bare skin between her hiking shorts and sock tops was cool, almost uncomfortable, but the feeling only lasted a few seconds and the breeze was refreshing. It did not take her long to have her backpack on, the book stuck in a side pocket, and headed for the trail that began up a steep incline through thick timber. After she walked several hundred yards she was hot and had to unbutton her over-shirt. After another hundred yards she stopped to adjust the straps to the backpack and catch her breath. "Maybe I won't walk as far today as I'd planned," she said.

After walking less than a mile her legs were already tight and sweat was running down between her shoulder blades. The back pack that had been light on her back in the living room seemed to gain ten pounds with each step. Sitting down heavily on a large boulder she leaned back against a pine tree and while slowly regaining her breath she spotted a woodpecker diligently pounding his beak into a rotted tree stump, his dark head moved back and forth like a miniature jackhammer and it made Sheila smile. She struggled back to her feet. "If you don't think about the pain it won't bother you," she told herself picturing in her mind an old Chinese sage walking barefoot across an endless desert in search of truth and wisdom.

After another hundred yards of the steep trail, she wanted to stop but forced herself on. "You always wanted to take me camping," she huffed. "Now I know why I didn't go."

She suddenly felt like crying, but held her tears. "I should have gone with you. I should have been with you more."

Trudging on, the image of her husband's smiling face came to her. He was holding three, six-inch long trout, but, by his smile and happy eyes, they were as big as a house. She fried them and they had eaten them with a tossed salad with a light vinegar dressing, washing them down with two bottles of white wine. Afterwards they made love and he told her about the mountain stream and how beautiful it was and how he wanted her to see all the beautiful sights as he saw them. "It would have been better with you there," he told her before he fell asleep with his head on her stomach.

Sheila stopped again and turned around. She could not see the parking lot, only the trail she had huffed along. The trail had not yet come out of the thick timber and she had not bothered to look around as she walked, more engulfed by her loss and physical pain. She fumbled in one of the side pockets of the pack and got out her topography map, more of an excuse to rest longer than to look at the map. She examined the elevation lines hoping there was a meadow close by where she could camp. "This could take me years," she said remembering Sylvia's words. "A camping trip for me is a suite in Vegas."

"Hell, it hasn't been two hours and I already want a hot bath and my shag carpet," she chastised herself.

Studying the map she noticed that if she had driven to the trailhead on the other side of the mountain, her hike would have started through the middle of a wide, level valley.

She continued on, trying to look around her, and absorb the trees, and not look down at the ground although it was easier to walk if she only looked at the ground. The pack straps were hurting her shoulders, but there was nothing she could do about it.

Feeling as though her legs could not go another step the trail leveled off and she entered a small clearing.

The sunlight was like walking into the lobby of a Hilton. The clearing was level and there were several patches of white flowers resembling miniature daisies. She let the pack fall heavily to the ground and plopped down beside it. After several minutes, she dragged the pack over to the edge of the trees. She figured she had gone no more than two miles but it was far enough. "You're not in as good of shape as you thought you were," she said as she rolled out her tent, "Pocahontas my ass."

It did not take her long to pitch her tent and roll out her bag and sleeping mat. She found a small stump and rolled it over to her tent for a table and picked several of the small flowers and stuck them in a crack in the stump. She leaned her pack up against the stump. Stepping back, her camp was beautiful in its simplicity. Her legs no longer hurt as much and, her shoulders, though sore, felt stronger. She spent thirty minutes picking up dead branches and carrying them back to her tent, and another thirty minutes bringing rocks to form a circle for a fire. When everything was in order, there were still several hours of light remaining. She did not want to sit down and tried to fight the feeling that she had to do something, anything. Over the past years she had never really been idle—when she was idle—she could not face her pain.

She decided to walk down the trail she had been on and try and see what she had missed on the way up. She felt as though there were springs on her feet without the weight of the backpack. As she back tracked she noticed ferns growing in damp areas and the way moss clung to the trees. Several chipmunks scolded her from the safety of a pile of boulders and she saw the footprints of a doe and her fawn. She had not noticed how noisy the forest was as she huffed up the trail, but now, she could hear the wind, the distant calls of unseen birds, the rumble of a stream and her own steady, rhythmic heartbeat. She stopped walking and shut her eyes. "I'm alone, but I'm not alone," she said. "I'm a part of all life, of all time."

She opened her eyes and headed back to her tent. By the time she had set up the small stove, hung the candleholder in the tent and picked out what she wanted to eat, it was getting dark. She used an entire book of matches to get a fire going, but she felt proud when the flames were established.

Later, sitting in the front of the tent, sipping on tea, eating noodles and chicken, with the firelight prancing off of her face and illuminating the clearing she thought of all the people sitting at home watching TV. Gazing up at the sky and at the millions and millions of stars she felt no bigger than a pebble or a snowflake—fleeting and insignificant. Sheila put another stick on the fire and poured another cup of tea. Looking deep into the shiny embers of the fire she could see his face. He loved to camp and begged her to go with him many times.

"No, you go. We each need our own space, our own time. We have to have our own interests," she told him each time he asked.

He always looked disappointed as he drove away with his fishing poles and gear wearing a ridiculous floppy hat with fishing lures attached to it. She always wanted to run after the car and say. "Wait, wait, I'll come." But, she never did.

The fire burnt down to a bed of red coals. The trees circling the clearing standing like silent sentries, large and ominous in their vigil. Timid field mice scurried through the tall grass avoiding the hot glare of the fire as they quickly gobbled seeds and bugs. The sigh of a horned owl filtered through the trees and got lost in the vastness. Sheila took off her boots and got into the sleeping bag. She lay peering into the dome of her tent where the faint glow of the stars made a night-light. Shutting her eyes she wanted to cry but she did not. There was no one to hold but herself.

The Mountain
<u>Once There Was A Great Bear</u>

In the 1930s and 40s there were reports of a gigantic grizzly bear on the mountain, but nobody took them seriously, as the bear was never seen by hunters during black bear season and everybody thought all the grizzlies had been killed in the state.

The first person to see the grizzly bear was a young man hired by a logging company to mark trees suitable for harvest. One hot summer afternoon in 1947 the man was tired and lay down by a dense thicket of alders. The man fell peacefully asleep but woke with a start, feeling terrified but not knowing why. As the man stood, a gigantic bear reared up on his back legs from the center of the alder thicket. The man screamed, too afraid to run. The bear roared and tore a path away from the man as wide as a truck. When the man finally calmed himself down, he went into the alder patch, and there, in the soft dirt, was a bear track as big as four of his hands, with claw indentions at least three inches long. Removing his undershirt and using the red paint for marking trees he drew an outline of the bears paw on his shirt.

That evening he showed his boss the drawing of the track. It caused quite a stir among the loggers who feared for their lives and in no time made the sheep and cattlemen nervous who grazed their livestock in the mountains during the summer. When the Forest Service was informed about the bear they were worried the bear might kill hikers and campers. Nobody took into consideration that the bear had beaten a path away from the logger as fast as his four giant legs could carry him.

The story of the bear spread over the entire state and two professors from the University came to investigate. After two weeks, they issued a statement to the press that the bear had to be a grizzly—the last known grizzly in the state. All the others had been shot for rugs, for the hell of it, or, because something so large and free had to be feared. The two professors began a campaign to have the bear made off limits to hunting. This caused such an uproar from hunters that the National Rifle Association lobbied for a special hunt to kill the bear. The cattlemen and sheepmen also offered a bounty for the bear although there was not a known case of either a cow or a sheep being killed by a bear. They did not care if the bear was shot during bear season or not, the money would be paid with no questions asked. An environmentalist group hearing about the bear started a campaign to stop all hunting in the area while making a small fortune selling T-shirts and sweaters with bear heads imprinted on them.

The bear knew nothing about all of this. He was simply trying to stay alive and find a mate. The bear was a male grizzly. His ancestors roamed the Rocky Mountains for thousands of years, fearing nothing except each other and an occasional brave Indian. During their thousands of years of being left alone, they had been the lords of their world. Large and solitary, they roamed the mountains eating berries and bugs, an occasional elk and deer they found dead, and sleeping peacefully through the long, cold winter.

When the white man came to the mountains with their rifles, and traps the size of wagon wheels, they killed the bears with wild abandon until there were no more grizzlies.

The grizzly was young when the only other grizzly in the area was killed. Hiding in thick brush he witnessed the man shoot the other bear, already half dead from the loss of blood from having his back leg caught in a trap. The bear knew he must fear this small creature with the desire to kill all it saw. From that day, whenever he would see or smell man, he ran away. As people began to invade the mountains in increasing numbers he moved to the most remote sections of the mountains, gorging himself during the summer on anything he could find, while searching endlessly for a mate. But, in his searching for a mate it was unavoidable for him to not make contact with man.

The years passed and he still searched futilely for a mate.

Word of the reward for the bear spread and hunters came from all over the country to try to be the one to shoot the gigantic bear. But none did. There were a few who saw a momentary glimpse of the grizzly as he crested a distant ridge or saw his large footprint. An occasional hiker saw the bear, but he was always running away so they were not afraid, but exhilarated from seeing something so ancient, so large and grand, almost prehistoric, a dinosaur in his own time.

The years rolled on and the bear still searched for a mate and avoided the hunters. But now the bear's back was covered with white hair and his teeth were worn down to nubs. His joints ached from arthritis and his senses of hearing and smell were almost gone.

Twelve years after the first sighting of the bear a rich hunter from Texas, who had killed animals all over the world, heard about the bear and was told about an Indian whose wife had died shortly after they were married. He had loved his wife so deeply he never remarried and lived alone in the middle of nowhere. The Indian was supposedly the best bear tracker alive and he did not use bait or dogs. The Texan wrote the Indian, who lived on the Jicarrilla Apache Reservation in northern New Mexico. The Indian had also heard about the bear and wrote back stating he would talk to the hunter about guiding him to hunt the bear, but only in person.

The Texan flew his airplane to Albuquerque and rented a car. When the Texan met the shriveled up old man in a bar in Lindrith, New Mexico, he had second thoughts about hiring him. The Indian was unwashed, at least seventy years old, skinny, not more than five feet five inches tall, and wore his waist length white hair in two long braids. He had only three teeth in his mouth. His brown face was one big wrinkle and the hunter knew immediately the Indian did not like him. "I will find the bear for you for free," the Indian told the Texan after the Texan had bought him three shots of whiskey. "Only you must give me the bones and the claws."

The rough looking Mexican bartender looked at the Texan while drying a glass, and said, "He is a drunk, but he knows bears."

With this encouragement, the Texan agreed, and a time was set to meet during the upcoming bear season. When the time came, the Texan met the Indian at a trailhead leading into the wilderness. A river separated the camping area from the wilderness boundary. The Indian drove to the trailhead in a dilapidated truck pulling a horse trailer, both held together with bailing wire. He brought two paint horses, two saddles that looked like they had been through a war, a few supplies in saddlebags, a couple of tarps, several ropes and no tent. On his belt he wore a large bone handled knife, with a piece of turquoise carved in the image of a bear set in the handle. He did not bring a rifle.

The Indian saddled the horses, got the gear together and they crossed the river into the wilderness. The Texan rode behind the Indian for a week. The Indian did not say one word to him. At night they ate a small dinner and slept fully clothed on the ground wrapped in tarps. At times the Indian would leave the Texan and be gone for most of the day. After nine days, the Texan was growing impatient and cursed at the Indian, but, the Indian only looked at him with sad, far-away eyes, and still said nothing.

On the night of the tenth day, the Indian and the Texan were sitting by a fire when the Indian said barely above a whisper, "Tomorrow you will shoot the bear. Make your aim good."

In the morning the Indian led the Texan, on foot, through trees so thick the light did not reach the ground and one had to walk sideways between many of the trunks. The timber was lifeless without even the sounds of birds or the skitter of mice. It made the Texan feel uneasy as if he were in a land populated only by lost souls. When they came to a narrow game trail, the Indian motioned for the man to hide off to the side of the trail behind a rotting tree. The man sat, his heart pounding in his ears, and tensely waited.

The Indian melted into the trees like he was a brother to the lost souls. The Texan waited less than an hour when he heard a tearing and crashing of branches that sounded like a herd of stampeding cattle. He stood and put the rifle to his shoulder, slipped the safety off just as the great white-backed bear appeared on the trail. Even with his fading eyesight the bear saw the man, but for some reason he did not turn and run but he slid to a stop. Saliva dripped from his mouth as he sniffed at the air and tossed his huge head from side to side. The Texan, so filled with awe at the size of the bear, did not pull the trigger. The bear let out a deep sigh and sat on his haunches.

The old Indian heard the shot and the thud of the bullet and he knelt down and wept.

Several hours later the Indian walked back to the grinning hunter who was sitting proudly by the dead bear. The Indian did not smile nor look at the man but went up to the bear and patted it gently on the head. Taking his knife the Indian gutted the bear, leaving the entrails on top of the ground for any creature that would dare to eat them. It took the men three days to haul the grand beast off the mountain on a travois pulled by one of the horses. The Texan rode and the Indian walked.

After they crossed the river and reached the trailhead, a cowboy was driving by and saw the dead bear. Within an hour, people from the small town in the valley along with ranchers and other hunters came to look at the magnificent grizzly. They talked and chatted excitedly.

The Indian, ignoring the people, cut the flesh away from the hide and bones and wrapped the bloody bones in an elk hide he had in the truck. He removed the claws and put them in a deer skin pouch. He cut the hide away from the skull. When he was finished he put his knife back in its sheath and removed his shirt and smeared a hand full of blood all over his chest and face and picking up the bloody bear skull, walked to the river. Standing in the middle of the river, with his back to the people, he held the bear skull above his head, with the empty eye sockets pointed at the distant mountain peaks. The townspeople, the hunters, and the Texan, watched the Indian silently. They looked at the lifeless, white-backed hide and pile of flesh and one by one they got into their trucks and cars and left. When only the Texan remained, the Indian, still holding the bear skull above his head, began to sing. He sang with a voice that was old and tired but filled with strength. The Texan could not understand the words the old man sang but he was entranced. The Indian sang and his legs grew numb from the icy water, and still he sang. He sang until the sun was about to set behind the mountains and then he staggered out of the river. With the dried blood still on his face and chest he put the bones and the skull in the back of his pickup truck, loaded his horses into the rusty trailer, then taking his bone handled knife with the turquoise bear in the handle he handed it to the Texan. He then left without saying good-bye.

The next morning, back at home, the Indian boiled the bones in water and brushed bleach on them. He faced the skull to the east on the brown dusty earth and circled it with the other bones. He strung the claws on silver wire with a small piece of turquoise between each claw and wore them around his neck.

Within a week, word spread about the death of the bear. Articles ran in newspapers about the history of the grizzly bear in the Rocky Mountains and after a month, a writer was sent to get an interview with the Indian for a national outdoor magazine. When the writer drove into the dusty yard of the Indian, he was appalled by the mud and stick one-room house where the old Indian lived. The house was surrounded by rock and sagebrush and twisted pinion and juniper trees that looked as though they were in pain. The writer could barely see the outline of the mountains in the distance. A few skinny goats with bells around their necks nibbled on whatever food they could find while three pathetic looking chickens darted in and around the dilapidated truck and horse trailer. But, not far from the house, set in a circle, were the bones of the bear with the skull in the center. The bones and skull were as shiny as ivory piano keys.

Getting out of his car the writer felt like he was stepping back in time and his new clothes and new car were an embarrassment to him. He stepped up to the Indian who was sitting on the porch. "I have come to ask you about the bear?" he said politely.

The old Indian looked at the writer, went into his house and came back with a 30-30 rifle. He pointed the rifle at the reporter and pulled back the hammer. The reporter, understanding completely, ran to his car and sped away. The Indian did not smile at his triumph.

That night the Indian sat on the porch and he sang all the old songs he could remember and he drank whiskey. He sang and he drank whiskey, but he did not drink enough whiskey to pass out. When he stopped singing the sun had not quite risen and a purple haze hung over the horizon. He wrapped the bear bones in his best blanket and walked toward the rising sun with his heavy load. After going more than a mile he set the bones down and started digging a hole in the ground with his bare hands. He dug through the rock and dry clay, ripping his fingernails and making his fingers bleed, but still he dug. He dug until the hole was so deep, the crafty coyotes would not go through the bother to dig them up. He put his blanket with all the bones into the bottom of the hole, placed the giant skull on top facing south, and pushed the earth into the hole with his bleeding hands. Soon the wind would scour the earth and no trace would ever be found of the grave.

Standing up slowly, the Indian gazed at the blazing sun, and then at the scarred earth and he said, "Now you will no longer be lonely," and he walked slowly back to his house and another bottle of whiskey.

Bill gazed into the fire. Gypsy lay by his leg; occasionally snapping at a cinder that blew close to her face like it was a troublesome bug. It was cool enough there were no mosquitoes, only a few brave moths that dived to their deaths in the fire, finding a plunge into hell better than living. Bill remembered her voice. "It's so beautiful Bill, I wish I would have come sooner."

Before that one time she would never go to the wilderness with Bill. They would go camping, but only to the, 'city-fide camping areas', as Bill called them. Those obscene places with designated camping areas equipped with barbecue pits and places to build a fire and forest service bathrooms stinking like a dead, bloated cow. Bill hated them, he hated them as much as he hated RV campers and pickup trucks with campers on the back, or those new nylon pop up tents that did not keep the rain out. But, he would go with her and they would sit around the fire at night in their fold out chairs and drink a few beers while listening to other campers and their blaring radios. "Why don't the bastards stay at home, hell, all they do is bring the city with them," he would fume, but still enjoying her.

"Some people don't know any better, Bill. To them this is camping. You wouldn't want them going back into the wilderness with their radios."

He would have to smile, knowing she was right. But even in his anger and disgust, he felt sorry for the people—people with their short pants and their few days away from the city. They had never been to the top of the mountain. They had never sat and looked out for hundreds of miles at the valleys and trees or watched the hawks soar. They had never fished for trout that were not dumped into lakes and streams by the forest service or seen an elk alone and free in a valley that took days to ride into on horseback. These people came to the mountains like they were going to a baseball game. They drank beer and ate hot dogs and left their garbage scattered everywhere. But, she liked it, and he loved her.

She never seemed to hear the noise, or even pay any attention to the other people. They were of no mind to her. He wished he could have been more like her, not so judgmental, not so angry, not such a hard person.

Gypsy darted off into the darkness, growling deeply as she ran. Bill listened to the bell. He hoped she was not chasing after a porcupine. When it came to porcupines Gypsy was about the dumbest dog he had ever had. He could not count the times he had to hold her in a headlock and pull quills out of her black nose. It was always a chore. The dog would cry and yelp and behave as though she was dying. But, if she ran into another porcupine twenty minutes after the agony of it all, she would have another face full of quills. Bill figured everybody had some kind of porcupine they could not stay away from.

Gypsy ran back and sat down by the fire looking brave and proud. "You didn't chase anything but your tail," Bill said to her.

Gypsy thumped her tail twice on the ground and looked away from Bill as though he did not know what he was talking about.

"I think I want to go to the wilderness," she told him one morning.

She was wearing an ugly pink bathrobe her mother had given her and her hair was up in curlers. Bill smiled, and replied. "Can't take your curlers."

"Can I go like this," she teased, letting her bathrobe fall open and exposing her nakedness.

They had made love on the kitchen table with Gypsy watching through the screen door. Afterwards, they talked about where he would take her. "Now I don't want to go anyplace that is a bunch of work, no tiny trails, no switchbacks as wide as your foot. I want to go on a nice easy ride, lots of flowers, a small stream, maybe a lake. I am not out to test myself like you are."

"I know just the place," he said to her. "Trust me."

She laughed her light, childlike laugh. "I trust you as far as I can throw you."

Bill put several small branches on the fire. For a moment he wished he had a drink. He pushed the urge from his mind. He drank heavily for the first year. It had done nothing but enhance the demons. The thought made him feel embarrassed, and weak, like one of those campers in his Bermuda

44

shorts sitting outside his RV thinking he was Daniel Boone.

Gypsy stirred. "Why don't you go find a porcupine," Bill told her, scratching behind her ears. The dog moaned, she loved her ears scratched.

"You're not worth a hoot," he said lovingly to the dog.

Bill got into his sleeping bag, looking at the stars through the swaying branches of the trees. "If I would have never wanted to touch the stars," he said and shut his eyes.

"The stars are so beautiful up here," she said. "I never knew there were so many."

"There are no stars without you," he told her.

"You only like me for my body," she said, taking his hand and kissing it.

Bill did not get out of his sleeping bag as the sun came up but lay listening to the birds as they greeted the day. It had been so long since he had been to the mountains he had forgotten how beautiful the early morning was.

A gray camp robber flew in and landed by the still smoldering fire. The bird looked at Bill, looked around the camp and flew away. Bill chuckled over the bird and got out of the sleeping bag. He could hear Gypsy's bell down by the stream. It did not take him long to catch the horses and load up the gear. When he started to ride, Gypsy appeared from nowhere and ran in front of him. Bill examined the sky and he was glad it was clear with no sign of a storm. He did not know if he could take a storm. It was hard enough as it was. As he rode, he tried not to think about the bones—the waiting bones.

The Woman
The First Camp

Sheila lay in her sleeping bag listening to the morning breeze rustling the tent, feeling like a little girl who had spent the night in her backyard in a tent she had made out of chairs and a sheet. All that was missing was her doll and the teddy bear her grandmother had made for her—the teddy bear with its large brown glass eyes that had always seemed so wide and caring. She grew melancholy thinking about her doll and teddy bear. She had not thought about them in years, although they were packed safely away in the attic.

Sheila had slept so deeply she had not dreamed or moved. Sitting up she found to her pleasure her legs did not hurt as much as she thought they would. When she crawled out of the tent, her little meadow was like a magical scene from the Wizard of Oz. She thought about all her friends who were speeding along the freeway, swigging coffee and listening to the radio to see what exit ramps were clogged or where there was a wreck. She started her propane stove and in a few minutes was sipping a cup of herbal tea. The sun was beginning to burn the dew off the grass and flowers. She looked sadly at the two wilted flowers she had picked and put on the stump and then at the living vibrant flowers growing in the meadow. "I won't pick anymore flowers," she said. "I feel like a murderer."

After she finished the tea, it did not take her long to roll up her tent and sleeping bag and pack everything. She made up her mind she would walk farther today. "You wimp," she scolded herself thinking about yesterday's meager walk.

Slinging the pack up on her shoulders and taking a deep breath she started out. She did not walk fast, but took her time, looking at the trees, the play of sunshine on the ground, the color of the rocks, and everything else that to her was quite foreign. "I don't know why I didn't bring a camera," she said.

Sheila had gone close to half a mile when she started to miss him. It was like it always was. She would be going along with her life and then she would miss him. She did not want to miss him, in fact, she really did not want to think about him. Not wanting to miss him was the main reason she went to the cemetery only once a year. She thought it might help, but so far, it had done little. She was not like other ladies she knew who had lost husbands. She did not keep photographs around the house. All the photographs had been tearfully packed away to a dark dusty corner of her closet. She wondered how the Chinese could place the ashes of their dead on the mantel, but then, she supposed the old photographs were like the ashes, even if she did not see them. "I don't want to miss you, don't you understand?" she called out, momentarily making the birds stop singing. "I want you to leave me alone. Please, leave me alone."

Sheila stopped, taking several deep breaths. The trail had started to climb again and she was in a stand of aspen trees. The light shone through the trees in intermittent circles of shadow and light. She was standing in the middle of one of the circles of light. "Beam me up, Scotty," she said. "Beam me up to a new world."

She started again and had a mental picture formed in her mind of the seven dwarves as they trudged off to the mine whistling and laughing. The image made her smile.

After about a half an hour she realized her mind had been blank. It was as though she had not existed. Her legs and feet had moved her to this point without her knowing it. The feeling made her feel both awed and strange. She did not know how she should react to the eerie feeling. It seemed in life one was always on guard, slightly paranoid or afraid of what another person might think about even the stupidest things. "Your slip is showing, you're not tanned, you're a little overweight, I never noticed those wrinkles on your forehead before."

She wished she had not stopped and was still reacting to life without knowing it. "It's all the thinking and planning that screws life up," she said.

Sheila thought about a book she had read, not remembering the title, but it stated the Indians of the old west did not kill crazy people. They believed crazy people could do no evil and therefore were blessed by God.

When she felt hungry she ate two high-energy granola bars. It was not until after she had eaten the granola bars that she heard the gurgling of a stream.

She came to where the stream crossed the trail. The stream was over twenty feet across but did not look over several feet deep. She stuck her hand in the water and shuddered. It was ice cold, bone chilling cold. She could see the large rocks on the bottom and realized she could not take her boots off to ford the stream. She clenched her jaw and stepped into the water. After only two quick steps, the cold made her legs hurt. In the middle of the stream, she stepped into a waist deep hole. The rushing water was like millions of tiny ice picks pricking her skin and made her gasp for breath. By the time she was on the other side of the stream her teeth were chattering and her legs were blue. She quickly removed her boots and socks and took off her pants and underwear. She felt as though every tree had six men behind it and quickly put on dry underwear and short pants. When she was done, she was elated and proud but she also felt like an idiot. "There are no men up here," she said as she sat down on a clump of dry warm grass. "Besides, maybe a man should see my naked butt."

The next thing Sheila knew, she was waking up. The sun was resting on top of a tall pine tree and her face was hot. She felt momentarily in a hurry. "I have to get to where I wanted to go," she mumbled. But then said, "Why? I don't have to be anywhere."

Looking at her topography map and then at the sun she decided she could make it to a clearing before dark. After putting on dry socks and her boots, she started off. She felt good, she felt strong, she felt brave.

The sun was setting when she made it to the clearing. In the graying light three deer darted into the dense trees. She was an invader. Pitching her tent next to a large spruce tree she rolled out her pad and sleeping bag. Putting a candle in her lantern and hanging it in the tent, she lit it, and was pleased at the way the tent lit up like a blue jack-o-lantern. In the fading light she quickly gathered several armfuls of dead branches. Clearing away a small circle she started a fire with only half a book of matches. She was standing by the fire as darkness took over the sky. Picking out the northern star she felt as though she could reach out and touch it. The star was like a friend, a long lost friend she had not seen in many years. "Twinkle, twinkle, little star," she whispered, as though the trees would ridicule her for acting like a little girl.

Sheila was so hungry she ate a complete dry meal and a package of dried apples. She sat cross-legged in the flap of her tent, sipping on a cup of tea and talking to herself. "Around the world there are wars, starving people, somebody sleeping in an alley, somebody shooting dope, somewhere somebody is being murdered, a lady is being raped. Here it is quiet and peaceful as though the other world is only a bad dream."

She put on a light jacket and made herself another cup of tea. "I'm lonely," she said to the fire. "I'm lost. But I'm also fortunate."

From somewhere deep in the trees, she heard an owl call out, and heard the soothing song of the wind as it traveled to another part of the world. A pack of coyotes howled. As she gazed deeper into the fire, it was as though she became one with it, and the trees, and the coyotes, and the owl and her blue tent with its candle for light.

After the fire burnt down, she got into her sleeping bag and blew out the candle. She zipped the bag up and covered her face. In the total darkness she started to cry. Soft, muffled sobs. Tears ran down her cheeks like warm raindrops, but nobody heard or cared.

The Mountain
Birth Of A Storm

Nobody knows for sure how many times the mountain has been reduced to a plain and then formed back into a mountain. Nobody knows for sure how many glaciers have scraped its sides and moved parts of its bowels to other far away mountains. There is evidence of many glaciers, there is also evidence of what geologists call ghost glaciers. A ghost glacier is an explanation for something that cannot be explained without a glacier being the reason, but, there is no evidence of a glacier. An example of a ghost glacier is a large boulder in the middle of a meadow with no scrape marks on it from ice, and there is no rock strata in the area from the same time period as the boulder. In many ways a ghost glacier is like the search for God.

What is known is that the mountain's original birth came from fire, volcanic fire. The mountain rose out of chaos and storms were its sculptor.

During the winter, most of the storms occurring on the mountain are snowstorms. Moist air blowing in from the west reaches the mountain peaks and comes down as snow. In what is portrayed in books and poems as beautiful and peaceful in all truth is violent and deadly. During the winter animals starve, rock cliffs crack and fall from the freezing and thawing, hillsides slip away, streams cut new beds and trees are uprooted. The storms timelessly change the face of the mountain.

During the summer, this same moist air builds up on the peak of the mountain. The seemingly harmless, white billowing clouds look like gathering snowmen. But, soon the clouds loose their whiteness and turn into black and gray caldrons of pent up force. When the thunder claps, it rolls down the mountain in ever crescendoing bellows, sending both man and beast for cover. After a thunderclap there is a profound silence as if every living thing on the mountain is deep in prayer. The thunder gives birth to the most violent and spectacular lightning on the face of the earth.

Lightning flashes spread out in jagged fingers of power—darting through the sky with dozens of squirming, lashing tentacles, and slamming into the ground with the force of small bombs. The lightning singes the air and taints the air with an acrid smell not unlike battery acid. Trees that have grown for hundreds of years, when hit by lightening, are either shattered into toothpick size pieces or they burst into flame. Cattle, only interested in the tall grass, when hit by lightning, will have their hooves blown off by the impact and become feasts for maggots and buzzards.

After the terrifying crashes of thunder and the sizzling daggers of lightning, advancing sheets of hail or rain march down the mountain like merciless barbarians. The hail is so fierce it will strip pine needles from trees and leave meadows so devastated they look like cattle have stampeded through them. The rain is bone chilling.

When the storms have passed the animals come out of their hiding like shell-shocked soldiers. The birds will not sing for awhile, afraid song will once again awaken the demon.

To nature's creatures, things destroyed in the storm are forgotten and life goes on with no remorse, but to man, one man in particular, they are never forgotten.

The Man
Sweet Memories

Bill's mind replayed a memory that was so vivid it was as though he was watching a movie.

"Why do you love the mountains so?" she asked.

Bill was sitting on the ground by the fire with a long stick in his hand, moving the logs around so the fire would flame more. She was sitting across from him on a folded tarp. The question settled over him like the circling darkness that the fire kept from engulfing them. He was silent for a long time, letting his mind ponder the question. She did not interrupt his silence. She had learned to be patient with him. "I don't know if I love the mountains," he finally answered.

He wanted to tell her how beautiful she looked as the fire danced off her face, but he did not. Remembering this small fact made Bill uneasy. It had always been hard for him to tell her he loved her—a fact which now hurt him deeply.

"You don't take people riding in the desert," she said, "so you must love the mountains."

"I don't like people," he replied.

She laughed her light dreamy laugh. "I know you don't like people, but you love the mountains. If it weren't for me you would be up here all the time."

"I enjoy being alone," he said, "but I miss you when I'm up here."

"You're nothing but an old sourdough cowboy. You don't need anybody."

"I need you. I try to tell myself I don't, but I do."

"I like it when you lie to me," she replied.

"I'm not lying," he said, feeling like a child.

"I know," she said softly, reassuring him, for such a tough guy he bruised easily.

"You love the mountains because it's the only place in the world where people can't tell you what to do," she said.

"The mountains are a joke," he replied angrily. "The mountains are like everything else in this world of ours, mapped out, trailed out and littered with beer cans and candy wrappers."

"I know, I know," she butted in. "There are no real cowboys left."

"I take it all too seriously," he said.

"You're no monk," she said.

"I have to get more wood," he told her.

When he came back, she was sitting by the fire with a blanket around her and had let her hair down. He put three logs on the fire.

"Are you a real cowboy?" she asked.

He did not have time to answer when she stood up and let the blanket fall from her shoulders. She was naked. "I like real cowboys," she said.

"Lady, I don't have any money," he told her, "but I sure like the view."

"You cowboys are all alike," she said. "Big on words but short on cash."

"I make good pancakes in the morning," he told her.

"Well, cowboy," she said. "Why didn't you tell me that sooner, this old cowgirl will do about anything for pancakes in the morning."

He carried her into the tent.

Bill was by the fire feeling hollow and empty from his thoughts. Gypsy ran in from the dark into the glow of the fire. She stunk. "Get the hell away from me," he ordered her while pushing her away with his boot.

Gypsy loved to roll in anything that smelled bad. She sat on the other side of the fire, looking at him as if saying, "if you would roll in a dead woodchuck sometime you might like it."

Bill stirred the fire. "How come I can't be like you? You old worthless dog," Bill said to Gypsy.

Gypsy perked up her ears.

"Why can't I get on with my life? Why can't I accept what happened?"

Gypsy whined and started to come over to him. "You stay away, you stinking dog," Bill ordered.

Gypsy sat, her smoky topaz eyes boring into Bill's.

Bill walked out into the darkness, far enough away so the fire did not wash out the stars. Gypsy waited until he was gone and then tinkled after him. Bill felt her standing by his leg before the stink reached his nose. He did not push the dog away but reached down and patted her head. "We stood here," he said to the dog. "We stood here and held hands and looked at the stars. We didn't talk. We held hands and looked at the stars. It was about the only time in my life I felt complete. I felt as though there was a reason or a purpose to life—it was as though all my life had led to that one moment, that one simple moment."

Bill patted the dog's head once again and gazed at the stars. They no longer gave him the feeling of wonder or hope. They were only there. He wanted to pack up the camp and ride back down the mountain. There was nothing here for him, nothing, only more emptiness, more longing, only bones.

Bill turned. The fire sent ghostly shadows out into the darkness. Camps at night had always made Bill feel good. "Candles in the darkness of night," he told her.

A statement that now sounded hollow, like some stupid poem one wrote to a high school sweetheart.

"Why do you love the mountains?" she asked him again after they made love.

"I love the mountains because they give me a reason to be a cowboy. They give me a job besides driving a truck or working in a feed lot. They let me show my life to people who only dream about the mountains."

They made love again.

Bill went back to the camp with Gypsy next to his leg. He scattered the fire and watched as the embers died down. Removing his boots he got into his sleeping bag. In the bag he smelled the stink of the dog, now on his pants. "I don't know why I keep you around," he told Gypsy.

Gypsy crawled onto the bottom of his sleeping bag, but he did not kick her off.

Dawn was several hours away when Bill got up. He started the fire and heated up the pot of coffee. When they were together, he had always gotten up first. He would sit in the kitchen drinking coffee and looking out at the dark. It was the best part of the day for him. A part of the day that was both lonely and hopeful at the same time. It had not been as lonely when he knew she was sleeping in the bedroom. When he was a boy on the ranch, he hated to get up. He hated it when his dad came into his room and made him get up. But when his dad was older and they knew they would lose the ranch, he always beat his dad up and Bill would be waiting in the kitchen for him. His dad was broken then, the ranch had been his life, and he was broken. When his dad died, it had been a blessing. Within six months his mother died. The world away from the ranch had been too much for her.

Sipping the coffee he thought about the war. The jungle. The heat. He thought about the beseeching faces of the children and their begging hands, as if a tin of rations or a piece of candy would ease their suffering. He thought about the whores, mostly young girls, selling their bodies on lice infested mattresses. He thought about the faces of the officers who yelled orders and ran around stumbling over each other like ants.

It was after the war he came to the mountains—the mountains had cured him. He had not been happy, but, he had been okay. The forest service officers left him alone. They knew he did not like them—anyone in a uniform he did not like. Uniforms signaled a man who wanted to tell people what to do or how to behave, as if they were gods and not tools for those in power. Bill hated those in power. He hated politicians, and mayors, game wardens and cops. It was not until he met her he discovered how much he hated, and what it had done to him. "I wish I'd met you earlier in my life," he told her the day they were married.

Now he hated the mountains. They had betrayed him and there was no room for forgiveness.

He pictured the meadow in his mind. The bones were there. He knew they were still there. Bones like beggar children's hands and whore's sad smiles. The bones were there. "Why do I have to touch the bones?" Bill beseeched the pre-dawn, "Why?"

Before the sun was up he packed up the horses and was riding up the mountain. Gypsy, before following him, went back to the rotting woodchuck, happily rolling on it.

The Woman
A Cold Bath

Sheila was sitting on a round, chalk colored rock and thumbing through her Rocky Mountain Flowers, Trees, And Mushroom book. She was trying to identify a flower that had many purple blooms that looked like tiny faces with hoods. She smiled when she found the colored photograph of the flower. "Monkshood, some species have been a source of drugs, and most are poisonous to humans and livestock. A European species of monkshood is the celebrated 'wolfbane' of werewolf lore."

When she was a little girl, the werewolf movies used to make her hide behind the sofa.

Standing, she realized her legs were not sore. In fact, her legs had firmed up and were tanned. She stretched out her arms and breathed deeply. "You need a bath," she said.

But thinking about plunging into an ice-cold stream did not appeal to her. As she started up the trail she had a memory of John, her high school boyfriend.

When he first went onto into the army, she was heartbroken. She could not eat, or sleep. There was no world without John. But, as the weeks passed, she discovered she really did not love him.

She wrote him everyday when he was in basic training. And wrote him every other day when he was in other training. When he got his orders she wanted to tell him she did not love him, but she could not force herself to do it, feeling he would need her letters over the next year. "I will wait until he gets back," she told herself.

Sheila never had to break up with John. His mother called her one afternoon—he had been killed. The helicopter he was in had crashed and all the boys were killed. Sheila felt sad, but she did not love him. At the funeral she cried, and then she went on with her life, but she was no longer a child.

Sheila passed through a stand of aspens. Off to the left of the trail a thick wall of red alders grew, so thick one could not see through them. She heard the faint bubbling of running water. Stepping off the trail her feet sunk into the deep layer of leaves. By the alders she smelled the earth scent of rotting vegetation and liked the scent. It reminded her of when she was a young girl and used to put rocks in her mouth and the taste was like the smell of rain on hot dry pavement. She pushed her way through the alders and on the other side found a crystal clear beaver pond. The dam made by the beavers was massive. Freshly chewed branches were sticking out of a beaver den and on the bank were footprints of the beavers and a small trough left by the beaver's tails when they crawled out of the pond. Around the pond, trees were chewed down and fallen across each other like pick up sticks. In the water she spied several small trout. Their sides were dark and covered with brilliant red spots. The pond had a different feeling than the forest—safe, hidden, secure in its veil of alders.

Sheila sat down on a sunny, grass covered slope. The sun beat down on her as though a blessing and she removed her backpack. Taking off her clothes and laying out her towels she basked naked in the sun. The cool breeze soothed her. After several minutes, she waded into the pool holding her biodegradable soap. The cold water jarred her at first, but, she gritted her teeth, squatted down and splashed water all over her back and arms. She lathered herself quickly and rinsed off. By the time she waded out of the water her teeth were chattering but she felt more alive than she had in years. She dried off and stood with the towel wrapped around her, feeling a tingling on her skin that could have been sexual but strangely, was more sensuous than mere sex. After she was warm, she put her towel down by the edge of the pond and kneeling on it, washed her hair.

When she was finished, she dried her hair as much as possible, put on clean clothes and sat in a warm sunny spot. Soon the forest forgot she was there and life began to move all around her. A grouse ignored her from an aspen tree. Blue and green dragonflies went skittering over the pond. She could see the rub marks on the alders where deer had cleaned the velvet from their antlers a year earlier—although she did not know what had caused it. The tiny fish cruised by the edge of the pond not more than a foot from her feet. Seeing the fish she was engulfed with sadness as deep and penetrating as the sunshine bathing her body.

His face always seemed so childlike when they ate the trout he brought back from his fishing trips. "I the mighty hunter," his male sense of provider declared proudly as they picked at the bony fish. His pride was so thick it covered her with a warmth as deep as a luxurious fur coat.

Sheila made her way back to the trail. He had been kind and gentle, loving and caring. He had brought her flowers and inexpensive earrings and chicken wishbones. But, what had love given her? Only a deep hurt, a pit of loneliness, a loneliness that gripped her even when she was brave, and made her afraid.

Several hours later the trail skirted another string of beaver ponds. It was so beautiful she decided to camp for the night. The ponds were in a long valley and each pond was connected by a stream that reminded her of a slow slithering crystal blue snake. She pitched her tent in a stand of pine trees where others had camped before—there was a circle of stones for a fire and a small pile of dried wood.

Sitting by her fire in the fading light, she saw two beavers swimming lazily along the edge of a pond. A brisk, cold wind swept through the valley and she put on her coat. Large dark clouds, made pitch black by the evening light, built up on the tops of the mountains and the dull thuds of thunderclaps sounded like approaching artillery shells.

By the time it was dark, a light steady rain was falling. The trees protected the tent and sitting inside under the pale glow of her candle, Sheila felt safe. She did not get into her sleeping bag for a long time but sat and watched through the open tent flap the distant lightning.

After getting in the sleeping bag, she wished he was beside her. He would not have had to hold her, or talk to her. He would only have to be there, sleeping, someone to reach out for during the night and touch. "Oh God," she begged. "Will I ever love again?"

The Man
The Hunters

In early fall, the animals living on the mountain are alerted. Loud echoing booms, usually in groups of three, roar up the canyons as hunter's sight in their rifles for the fall hunts. A few hunters will seek out black bear and fewer yet will put in for the limited number of big horn sheep tags that are issued by the state through a lottery—but most hunt deer or elk.

For the animals, the fall used to be the time to graze and browse and try to gain enough weight to survive the long, bitterly cold months ahead. It is now weeks spent in hiding and fear.

There is nothing wrong with hunting. Man is and will always be a hunter, whether it is for the stars or for animals. Perhaps what is saddest about modern day hunting is not the hunter but the state of hunting. Deer and elk herds in the west must now be managed because their natural habitat has been reduced to a pathetic level. Without hunters' kills, many animals would starve to death during the winter.

A day before the hunting season starts, the mountain roads become a parade of jeeps, pickup trucks and campers. Stowed in the trucks are lanterns, tents, gas cook stoves, air mattresses and tent heaters. Those with campers bring the city with them.

Stuffed into these metallic horses sit men, who on the most part, spend the rest of the year sitting in an office, dreaming about the few days they will spend in the mountains—dreaming about the stars and the trees and the smells that their ancient ancestors took for granted. By coming to kill, they try to find favor with the earth. Inwardly, they know everything else in their life is a falsehood.

The men, and a few boys trying to be men, dress in heavy pants, boots, sweaters, and hats; most of the clothing is colored red or orange. It is the law.

The hunters have rifles that can place a two hundred-grain slug in the middle of a pie plate two hundred yards away, some even five hundred yards. To most, the art of tracking is lost. One does not learn the habits of animals by watching hunting shows or videotapes. For most the mountain is more alien than the moon would be. They are only bit part players in a movie. The hunt is the fantasy; the man-made real world has become the reality.

The majority of the campsites on the mountain are full by late afternoon the day before the hunt. But, even after dark, more hunters will arrive, having left their work in a panic, only to set their camp in a panic. In truth, these people have grown so used to their life's fast pace that to be anything else but in a panic might be suicidal.

At night campfires will dot the mountain like the fires of an ancient army waiting for the dawn's assault—only—this enemy cannot fight back, it can only flee, or hide in areas so difficult to reach a hunter will not enter.

Around the fires, men will tell stories of other hunts while passing beer or whiskey or drinking coffee that tastes better than home perked coffee. Boys, allowed to join the men, will sit as though in a trance, pulled by the magic of the fire and the boasting and laughter of the men. The boys not yet fleeing the world, they are still exploring, searching, too young to have had their dreams destroyed or understand how small the mountain has become.

On the mountain, the deer or elk have heard the noise and commotion, and know what is happening. The wise old bucks will go to areas that have served them well in past years. A deer or elk does not grow old with his majestic rack by standing in a meadow on the first day of hunting season nibbling on the slightly frosted fall grass.

In the morning, long before the sun comes up, men will spill from the campers and tents, reheat coffee and fill pockets with candy bars and snacks. They will stand like mute sentinels until the eastern sky turns pale and then march out into the woods. Some energetic souls will already be sitting on ridge tops or hidden beneath the branches of a tree by a game trail. As soon as the sun clears the horizon a series of shots will blast through the icy air as though a guard is firing at an escaping prisoner.

By the end of the day, many camps will have deer or elk carcasses hanging from trees and the hunters will be frying liver and onions. The ones lucky enough to get their prey on opening day may now enjoy the remaining days of the hunt. While the others trudge off in the morning, he will sleep in, waking to the sound of the birds or the music of a nearby stream. During the day he will sit and listen to life and feel sad at times. Sad enough he will hide the truth from himself beneath another layer of responsibility or dreamed up needs.

When the last day of the hunt is over, campers and trucks and jeeps will file off the mountain like an army convoy. These convoys will be stopped by game wardens that have set up roadblocks to find those who have shot illegal game or do not have a hunting license.

As the hunters near their city homes, they will be somber. Sitting in bathtubs and taking showers, they will wash away the smell of smoke and the scent of pine needles. They will shave off the beard growth and pat on after-shave and the mountain will be gone for another year.

Several days after hunting season no conversation rolls up the mountain, no rifle shot rings out followed by its deathly silence, as if for a few seconds all living things have died. The survivors slowly come out of hiding—hungry and thirsty they take tentative steps to the edge of clearings—sniffing the air for the man smell that has now been blown away. Coyotes feast on the guts of field dressed animals, yapping and chasing away the boisterous ravens and crows that fly in for their share of the bounty. Clouds of giant skin headed buzzards circle the sky waiting patiently for their share. The true sounds of the mountain return.

In the late fall, after camping and hunting season and before the heavy snow storms, there are a few who venture to the mountain. Now there is only the mountain and what lives on the mountain. These few come alone to fish the deserted streams or walk the abandoned trails.

In the browned out valleys only dried stems remain of the wildflowers and grasses. In the early morning the valley floors are glimmering fields of ice crystals as if thousands of fairies have flow over sprinkling their magic dust. The deer and elk, no longer afraid, fill the lower meadows, and stand looking at the solitary figure as he moves by. Mountain sheep clatter on lower rock cliffs, no more alarmed than domestic goats. These late fall campers are the true hunters. They do not search for the fantasy. They know what is real. It is why they are alone. The mountain accepts them. They bring only silence.

The Man
Learning To Dance

Bill was leaning against a large boulder composed of millions of multi-colored pebbles held together by what had once been an oozing sea bottom. Gypsy was resting at the base of the boulder. The boulder perched on the edge of a canyon like a lone sentinel far away from the safety of his army. The canyon was at least one thousand feet deep and over a quarter of a mile wide.

On the horizon the mountains stretched out like a low-lying bank of dark clouds moving in on a seaport town. All that was missing was the squawking of pleading gulls. On the opposite edge of the canyon rim, following a trail that cut in and out of trees, Bill saw a pack string. There were four riders. A man with a white cowboy hat led while behind him were two riders, who, by the way they rode, Bill knew were paying guests. Behind them, another cowboy rode, followed by two packhorses.

Bill watched the pack string until it turned away from the canyon rim and then went back to a rolling meadow of grass and blooming wildflowers to his hobbled horses. As he mounted, Gypsy ran up the trail to where Bill could not see her.

"I believed in the war," Bill said to the back of the horse's head. "I was young and I believed. We were the saviors of the world. The country that God had blessed. The country that was right in all things. When I came back home I didn't think anything would be different—but it was never the same. Seemed I couldn't get along with anybody, didn't want to get along. All I wanted was to be alone."

Bill heard the drumming of a grouse's wings, but did not see it as it flew through the timber. "I don't really remember much about the war now. I don't remember much about the years following the war. It's been so long it doesn't seem real. Nothing seems real."

The horse swished his tail at a sweat bee hovering on his rump. "If

I would never have met her, I would never have known what feeling alive was," he said.

"You can't fool me," she said after they had dated a few weeks. "You try to act as though nothing matters in the world. You ride your horses and wear that tough look, but I know you Bill."

He tried to act tough, tried to ignore the remark. She only laughed. Laughed and stepped up to him and he was holding her before he knew what his arms were doing. Holding her and pulling her warmth into his insides and his heart.

"If the world is what we wanted then we would not need," she said with her head resting on his shoulder. "God makes it so tough so we can love."

She taught him how to laugh. Something he had once again forgotten how to do, or would not allow himself to do.

But why should he laugh now? She was gone. His life was gone.

"I am the Tin Man," he said to the horse.

"You're taking me dancing," she said after they dated several months.

He squirmed like a little boy, looking for excuses.

At the dance hall, he felt like everybody was looking at him, laughing at him. "People are only here to have fun," she said as she led him to the dance floor. "They have their own problems."

"I can't dance," he said, the sweat running down his back.

"If you're going to sleep with me you're going to learn how to dance," she smiled at him.

He learned how to dance. He could dance the Two Step, the Cotton Eyed Joe, the Shaddish, and the Western Waltz. And he learned how to laugh. Dancing with her had been like dancing with the wind.

"On Saturday we would go dancing," he said, feeling the emptiness return.

An emptiness like a cold river stone resting in the middle of his chest. A stone so cold and heavy there was nothing that would make it go away. Not even a river in flood.

"Have you ever been on a vacation?" she asked.

"The mountains are always a vacation," he replied.

"You've never taken two weeks off and just gone somewhere?" she said, unbelieving.

"Never thought about it," he said.

"We are going to take a vacation. There is more to life than work."

He tried to think of excuses, but there were really no good ones. A man came and fed the horses. A cowboy friend took over his pack trips and they flew to San Francisco for a week. She was radiant. They went to the museum, sipped drinks by the ocean and made love underneath the Golden Gate Bridge engulfed by the fog and the blaring cry of the foghorn. They took a limo tour of the wine country and sipped wine and ate breadsticks. When he kissed her, her lips were sweet and sticky. When they returned, for the first time in his life he knew there were many things in life he was missing. There was a whole world out there. A world filled with different people and different places. People who did not think like him, dream like him or even care about horses. On his next pack trip he enjoyed the mountains more than he ever had.

It was years before she asked him to take her to the mountains. He remembered how happy he was when she asked to go. She would see his world. A world that clung to the old. A world where one did not have to kiss the boss or put on a suit. A world where a man was still a man and not some dressed up dummy that nodded his head. "It's how man is supposed to live," he told her.

"You would have been a good Jesse James," she said.

Bill hollered to the treetops. "Why, God?"

The horse's head jerked, shocked from some distant daydream of open pastures and no saddles.

"You tease us," Bill yelled. "You give us bits and pieces of life that are good and then You take it away and want us to go on. Go on to what?" he sneered. "Go on to lies and false promises."

Bill pulled back on the reins, stopping the horse. He turned the horses and started down the trail at a medium trot. For five minutes he sat grim-faced and stern, holding his weight on his heels to cushion the bounce of the horse. Gypsy ran behind the horses. Bill suddenly yelled out, "You bastard," and skidded the horses to a stop.

The packhorse rammed into the back of Bill's horse, his eyes wide and filled with fear. Both horses breathing deeply. Gypsy barked and continued to run down the trail.

Turning the horses Bill started back up the trail. Gypsy ran back to him seemingly confused. "I need the bones," he cried out. "I'm no coward. I need the damn bones."

Gypsy, lowering her tail, slinked away into the forest.

The Woman
The Unanswered Wave

A gray fox squirrel sat on the lower branches of a pine tree, holding a pine cone in his small front hands like an ice cream cone. He would nibble on the pinecone, stop, look over at Sheila, twitch his tail showing his agitation and then nibble on the pinecone once again. Sheila had heard that squirrels, at times, carried plague infected fleas and pondered how a creature so cute could be a killer.

The squirrel, tired of being bothered, flicked his tail, barked loudly and scampered higher into the tree.

Studying her topography map Sheila knew that within two days she would be at the meadow she had picked as her destination. The thought of reaching the meadow did not make her elated, but rather morose, feeling she wanted her hike to go on forever.

She started on her journey once again. Now, after several days of hiking, she was a different person. When she woke in the morning, she did not rush around and think about what she should wear to work or how many appointments she had crammed into her day. She did not have to force a smile at an obnoxious customer or kowtow to a banker who sat behind his desk with a bored look on his face like some over bloated Buddha of money. Her life had become: Will it rain? How far will I walk today? And, is this a pretty spot to camp? She had even dismissed the idea of searching for mushrooms. She did not want to search, she only wanted to be.

She pictured herself thousands of years in the past. She was sitting around a fire with members of her tribe. Her baby was resting on an animal hide by her feet. She thought of herself running off to work with her panty hose and high heels and had to laugh at the comparison.

Sheila went around a sharp bend in the trail and was on the edge of a deep canyon that was about five hundred yards across. The canyon extended past her eyesight and was too steep to descend. Sheila looked past the canyon rim toward the mountaintops. To her, there was something alien about the treeless tops of mountains. Something that should not be reached or searched for, as if finding it would chill her heart with a truth that could never be overcome—a truth that would take all remaining hope from her.

Sitting, an urge swept over her that made her skin tingle. She wanted to take off her clothes. She wanted to be kissed all over her body. She wanted her nipples to be hard as small stream pebbles and her thighs ache with desire. She wanted to feel the flesh of the man she had loved cover her, rub her, stroke her. She wanted to buck and thrash like a wild horse and scream out. She wanted to lay in his arms, both of them panting, and listen to his heart race and slow up, until it was a steady beat like a tom-tom guiding the feet of pagan dancers.

"You selfish bastard," she said, her words carried away by the wind. "You die on me and you leave me alone, you selfish bastard."

Sheila shut her eyes. "After you died I could not even look at a man for awhile," she said to the darkness behind her eyelids. "Then I was so lonely I started to date."

She smirked. "I don't know why I dated, really. Maybe it was because I felt it was what I was supposed to do? You know. Go and search for a new life, be free, be independent."

She remembered some of the men she had slept with. The unfeeling fondling as if she was some wench from a bar—the smell of alcohol and the touch of warm skin that gave no warmth. The feeling of guilt she had afterwards, as if she had stolen something from the men, or worse yet, they had stolen from her. "I don't bother now," she said, opening her eyes. "I don't want to use or be used."

Standing, a movement on the opposite edge of the canyon caught her eye. There was a man on a horse wearing a cowboy hat with a pack horse behind him and a German Shepherd running along the trail in front of them. The man was riding slowly, his shoulders relaxed like he had ridden thousands of miles. It was as though the man, the dog, and the two horses were all one creature. A creature filled with diversity but still one—one heart, one mind, one soul.

The man's head moved, the white cowboy hat bright against the green of the canyon side, and he looked straight at Sheila. Standing on her tiptoes she smiled and waved hello. The man looked away from her and did not wave back. "I know you can see me," she called.

The dog stopped, looked directly at her and barked, and before continuing on looked at the man. The man glanced toward Sheila and she waved once again, but, he quickly turned away as if seeing her frightened him and once again he did not wave back.

Sheila, dejected, sat down in front of a twisted, dead stump—its roots spreading out like old people's gnarled fingers. "I don't want you wave to me," she said to herself.

But, she did not stop looking at the man. And, it was as though she was holding a magnifying glass up to her eye and could see the man close up and also feel what he was feeling. She could see the distance in his eyes and feel the great longing in his heart and she wanted to reach out and touch him. It was as though he was riding in a great void where only he and she existed. She stood and called, "Hello."

Hello, hello, hello, echoed through the canyon.

The dog stopped and looked at her once again but the rider did not take his eyes off the trail.

"I bet your hands are rough," she said after a few moments. "I bet you are strong and at night when you take your boots off, your back hurts and your legs ache. I bet you are quiet, and do not like to talk about yourself, and you take your hat off when you talk to a woman. I bet you have been in fistfights and have come home so drunk from whiskey you could not find the door."

The dog ran back to the man and she heard him call her Gypsy. "You can hear me. If I can hear you, you can hear me and see me," she hollered, getting angry.

But, even upset she wanted to know what color his eyes were and if he smiled when he talked. The dog barked and ran up the trail. "You are a real cowboy," she said quietly, and her words made her sad for some unknown reason.

She laughed a sarcastic chuckle thinking about all the men in town with their expensive cowboy boots who strutted around thinking they were cowboys—men who had never ridden a horse. She thought of the new dancing establishments with saddles and chaps hanging on the walls, while colored lights illuminated the men and women with blow-dried hair and matching outfits dancing to the latest popular songs.

"Why are we lonely?" she asked the distant rider.

The cowboy glanced at her again and she waved but again he did not wave back. There was no return of warmth. No return of longing. "Hello," she called again.

Hello, hello, hello, echoed once again through the canyon.

The man disappeared around a bend in the trail. "Good luck," she hollered. "I hope you find what you seek."

Walking on, she could not get the sight of the man and his horses and dog out of her mind. "You bastard, you uncaring bastard," she spat.

Gazing at the canyon rim she felt as though she had lost an opportunity in her life she would never have again. A magic moment had passed because of an unanswered call and wave. "You selfish son-of-a-bitch," she hollered. "You are not the only one who needs."

The dog's bark echoed faintly back to her.

The Mountain
The Outlaw Iron Joe

Iron Joe is what the old timers called him, although all the old timers who had met Iron Joe or said they had met him are long buried. But their descendants still talk of Iron Joe and tell his story.

The first white people that came to the mountain were trappers. Solitary men, they braved the weather and the Indians for pelts. When the beaver were all gone and the trappers were either killed by Indians or each other, the second people to come to the mountain were miners looking for the mother lode. Neither of them came for the fishing or the hunting or the view. They came with a consuming dream of riches which few of them ever realized.

Modern man quests after riches in the mountains of Wall Street and big business. Most, like the trappers and miners, do not fulfill their dreams and lose more than their lives along the way.

After the miners, people who came from the east started a small town at the base of the mountain. These people were clerks and storekeepers. They did not seek freedom but conformity, as if conformity would end the chaos of life. They established banks and schools and made laws.

Rich European investors bought up the land around the small town, built fences and created cattle dynasties, a few remaining to this day.

With the towns and ranches, the mountain became the last place for the disenchanted—a sprawling beacon for those who, by choice or need, could no longer live within the confines of a town and its laws.

Iron Joe was one of these people—he was an outlaw. Those who met him said he was always polite and laughed a lot but his eyes were snake eyes—cold and calm. Iron Joe wore one black handled 44/40 pistol on his hip and carried a double-barreled ten gauge shotgun in the crook of his arm and a 45/70 Craig in a scabbard on his saddle. Nobody ever saw him kill a man but there are tales he killed men from Kansas City to Denver. None of them shot from the front but blown into small pieces from a shotgun blast to the back. Iron Joe knew how to live to an old age. He also knew how to shoot a shotgun.

Iron Joe liked to rob stagecoaches and he was good at it. He never had a gang and he never shot a driver or a guard. Sadly for him, most of his stickups did not make him enough money to be a really high-class outlaw.

Iron Joe built a two-room cabin on the mountain. He had a half-breed woman and three black stallions that could outrun the wind. When Iron Joe finally met his end, the half-breed sat on the edge of town, slashed her wrists, and wailed for three days. At the end of the three days she left, nobody knows what happened to her, but they never forgot her wails.

Iron Joe, being the good outlaw that he was, never bothered the people in town or robbed a stage in the area. He knew one did not make trouble in his own backyard. Because of this, the people, who did not make it a habit of wanting to know everybody's business, left him alone. Having an outlaw in the area had its own amount of class. Iron Joe was not Butch Cassidy, but, he was an outlaw and every rancher or farmer or store keep who spent his life breaking his back for little or nothing has always respected a man with the strength not to give in and who was not a horse thief.

Everybody for miles knew where on the mountain Iron Joe lived. Even the local Sheriff. But, the Sheriff also knew how to grow old and minded his own business. In those days, laws were enforced when they needed to be—not to bolster egos or as a crutch or as government control. Most people could still take care of themselves. Calling on the law was considered a weakness.

Things were going fine for Iron Joe until he robbed a stagecoach carrying a mine payroll and was recognized by the guard. The robbery angered the mine owners and surprised Iron Joe who made so much money he did not know what to do with it. The mine owners bankrolled a posse and a three thousand dollar reward was offered for Iron Joe, dead or alive. With money on their minds the posse rode to the town at the base of the mountain.

The people in town liked the money the posse spent at the store and the bar as they prepared to go get Iron Joe, but they really did not like the idea of rich mine owners. Nobody knows for sure who rode up to Iron

Joe's to warn him, but the story goes when Iron Joe was informed there was a posse in town wanting him dead or alive, he only smiled and muttered something to the effect of, "Hell, I always know'd how it would end. I ain't no fool," and he gave the man a hundred dollars in gold coin.

Iron Joe sent his half-breed into the woods, barricaded his cabin, made sure all his guns were loaded and waited for the posse.

When the posse surrounded his cabin, a lawman on the mine payroll, with the top of his head sticking above a fallen tree, hollered at Iron Joe. "Iron Joe, you come out of there, you ain't got a snowball's chance in hell."

The man's warning was met with a rifle slug that tore the top of his head off. Being a good outlaw Iron Joe did know how to shoot and shooting a man who would hunt people down for rich people did not seem like a crime to him. It was more like shooting traitors.

For three days, the posse fired enough lead into Iron Joe's cabin to sink a ship. But Iron Joe had built his cabin with thirty-inch thick logs and rifle slots instead of windows. The posse became so infuriated, they shot Iron Joe's three black stallions. After three days it was Iron Joe three, posse zero, unless you count horses, then it was tied.

On the night of the fourth day, the posse managed to set fire to Iron Joe's cabin and proudly watched as the fire turned into an inferno. "We warned him," said one man.

But, Iron Joe had built a tunnel under the cabin that went underground for over a hundred yards. He let the fire grow so hot he could hardly stand it and then scurried through the tunnel, coming out by a large boulder behind the posse Iron Joe took off on foot.

In the morning, drunk from celebrating and counting and recounting their yet unclaimed reward money, the posse walked up to the ashes of the cabin. It was a sobering fact when they found no charred remains of Iron Joe and discovered the tunnel.

The posse scoured the mountain for a week without finding a sign of Iron Joe or his half-breed. When they rode off the mountain they did not stop in town. People were glad to see them go and glad to not see Iron Joe draped over a saddle.

It was six years later when the half-breed sat on the edge of town, slashed her wrists and wailed for three days. When she was done she left a letter lying on the ground where drops of her blood had dried dark black on the dry earth. A small boy picked up the letter and, quick as a young rabbit, ran to his mother. "The sad lady left it," he told her breathlessly as he gave her the letter.

She opened the letter and read. 'I never hated no man. I never kilt no man who didn't deserve to die. I never stolt from the poor. I was old. You tell the government bastards I kilt myself. There ain't no freedom left. Pity the children. I'm glad to be dead.'

The letter was signed, 'Iron Joe', with a P.S. 'I buried my gold on the mountain.'

"What did the letter say mom?" the boy asked.

"It said a man with a good heart died," she answered.

After the boy had gone back outside to play, the lady sat staring out the window. She was silent for a long time. After awhile, standing, she ran her hands over her dress and murmured, "I wonder if someone will wail for me?"

The woman put the letter in her jewelry box. She lived to be ninety four—had two husbands, seven children and sixteen grandchildren. When she died, the letter was found with her inexpensive jewelry and made its way to the boy who had picked the letter up and was now a seventy four year old man living in Denver. The man was a veteran of World War I and had lost a son in World War II. One day, after rereading the letter, he went to a small corner bar, where, between glasses of beer, he told the story of Iron Joe to two strangers. When he was done, all the men raised their glasses. "Pity the children," one of the strangers said solemnly.

After the toast, the men were quiet for a few moments until the man said. "I know what's wrong with this world."

"What?" one of the strangers asked.

"There ain't no good outlaws left," the man answered. "Now we are all just a bunch of crooks."

No trace remains of Iron Joe's cabin on the mountain. The mountain still has the gold.

The Man
Riding The Storm

Large, violent, dark clouds were building on the horizon and Bill quickly set up camp in the dark timber trying to stop the visions of flashing lightning that darted through his mind, making his heart race in fear. He knew the timber was the safest place to be if a big storm blew in. He remembered her watching the storm advance. "It's so beautiful," she said.

He long-lined the horses between two trees, not wanting to leave them in a meadow. Bill did not like the gloom of the dark timber. The musty smell of rotting leaves and decaying wood was a place animals would go to die. The birds did not even like the dark timber. All life gravitated to the sun and the open. Only fear brought one to the realm of shadows.

With his tent pitched, Bill gathered wood for a small fire and barely made it back to the camp when the first drops of cold rain pelted the tent. He sat on his sleeping bag trying to quell his fear as the storm grew in intensity. A clap of thunder rolled down the mountain and Bill thought about the woman he had seen earlier in the day. "I wonder why I didn't wave back?" he asked Gypsy, who huddled, shaking, by his feet—she was also afraid of storms.

Bill had heard the lady's words echoing down the canyon. They sounded like the cries of a person lost at sea—crying out in vain at a distant ship disappearing over the horizon. "I should have waved and called back," he said, feeling both guilty and lonely.

Gypsy ignored him.

Bill had seen the woman long before she waved. Objects not a part of the forest stuck out to Bill. He could pick out the outline of a deer's ear from thick brush and after years of guiding, could look at a hillside, not focus on any one object and see the minute details of the entire hill. The lady's bare legs stuck out like a hunter's orange jacket. "I bet she was smiling until I didn't answer," he said to Gypsy.

Bill was suddenly afraid for the woman. She might camp where it was dangerous during a storm, she might get lost, every bad scenario possible ran through his mind. Not far away a bolt of lightning slammed into the ground. Bill began to sweat. "Go to a low place," he beseeched the woman. "Don't camp underneath a lone tree. Please?"

Bill thought about how pretty the lady was. He pictured her with her short pants and tanned legs and how the breeze jostled her auburn hair. "I wonder why she was alone?" he asked.

Most people went into the woods with another person, a fact that was a good idea. "She's brave," he said.

"I should have waved and called back," he told the dog once again feeling sad.

Gypsy jumped as another bolt of lightning slashed through the sky. The rain pounded on the tent. Gypsy put her muzzle on Bill's leg. He began rubbing the dog's head. "Is she safe?" he asked Gypsy.

Bill heard the tree tops groan from a powerful gust of wind. He wondered where the woman was from? For some reason he wanted to be with her now. They could talk. Talk about anything. It would be nice to meet her and sit around a fire and talk.

He could see the lady sitting in one of those light back packing tents that leaked water. She would be nibbling on a granola bar or eating one of those prefab meals outdoor shops made a fortune on. She would like the storm. It would be exciting to her as the sky filled with slashing flames— everything lit up like quickly vanishing fragments of dreams. She would be sitting barely inside the flap of her tent, feeling like she was part of the storm and the mountain—not truly understanding the danger.

"I should have answered her. Waving back would have made me feel happy," he said. "I should be able to be happy at times."

Standing he looked out the flap of the tent. The wind had stopped along with the rain. He knew the brunt of the storm had missed him. He felt relieved for himself and the lady and his body and mind relaxed.

Bill rummaged around in his gear and dug out two cans of Vienna Sausage and crackers. He fed one to the dog and ate one himself.

After eating he checked the horses. Gypsy ran by him, the tinkling bell cutting the eerie silence of the dark timber.

It grew dark and Bill got into the sleeping bag. He wished the woman was with him in the sleeping bag. He wished he could reach over and hold her close to him. He wished he could tell her, "I should have waved. I'm sorry. Next time I will."

As he began to fall asleep he felt uneasy, as though a dear friend was moving far away and saying good—bye, both knowing they would never see each other again. "I'll never have another chance to wave to her," he muttered.

Beyond the dark timber, the stars shone brightly. The air was fresh. The meadows would be a vibrant green in the morning. The bones would be washed and shiny as ivory.

In dream Bill heard the calls from the woman, like pleas for help, "Hello, hello, hello," and he knew he had made her sad and it also saddened him.

The Woman
Kissing The Storm

Sheila set up her camp in a clearing with a magnificent blue spruce growing on its edge. It struck her as a particularly beautiful campsite. After everything was in order she decided to go for a walk, there was more than enough light left. Walking without her pack, she felt light on her feet and was not paying any attention to the sky when a cold gust of wind groaned through the trees. Within two minutes, the sky was a churning mass of gray and black. The clouds alarmed her and she started back to her tent at a brisk pace. Lucky for her, the storm did not hit until she was sitting inside the tent.

When it did hit, the nylon tent was savagely buffeted by the wind. When the rain started, interlaced with bright flashes of lightning, Sheila felt as though all her senses were turned up a degree. Sitting by the flap of the tent, splattered by the rain, she was fascinated by the fury of the storm. The gray and black clouds raced across the sky as if challenging each other. Images ranging from contorted faces filled with fury to darting birds formed in the clouds. When the thunder boomed, it shook the ground and when the lightning flashed, it was as if a flare had been dropped from an airplane.

Sheila was transfixed by the power and fury of the storm and thought of the cowboy. She wondered how many of these storms he had ridden through? She wondered where he was now? For some reason she did not understand she felt secure that they were on the same mountain. He would be in his tent, as she was, both alone, connected by their separation.

The storm intensified and Sheila shut the flap to the tent. Droplets of water dripped through the nylon tent.

As it grew dark, she lit her candle lantern, placing it on the floor of the tent, afraid to hang it in the swaying tent. "I wonder, if I had been walking on the trail he was on, would he have talked to me?" she asked herself.

"I bet he would have talked to me," she said, momentarily confident.

"I bet he would have had to force himself not to laugh."

"He probably hates hikers," she mused. "He hates people who come up here like rats escaping from the city to ruin his solitude."

Sheila got a granola bar out of her pack. "I bet he hates granola bars, too," she said, taking a bite out of the bar.

"I bet for breakfast he fries greasy bacon with eggs and has pancakes covered with syrup and drinks coffee that is so black you can see the future in it."

She laughed, suddenly hungry for bacon and wishing she had a cup of coffee and not herbal tea. "If he knew I had herbal tea, I know he wouldn't talk to me."

The wind stopped suddenly and the silence that followed was eerie. Sheila went outside and the sky was ablaze with millions of stars. Looking at the stars she wondered if there was a creature on another planet somewhere in the endless vastness that was camping and looking out and feeling the same as her. The thought made her shudder—she crossed her arms around her stomach and held herself. The large blue spruce on the edge of the clearing stood out like a silent guard, and she imagined druids in long dark robes with hoods covering their faces so no one could see their eyes, circling the tree and chanting a prayer for the earth.

"Do you pray cowboy?" she asked. "Do you sit on your horse and feel the earth slipping away? Are the mountains only a park now? A relic like the dinosaurs. Have we turned you into a living relic? Something to look at and wonder over and feel sorry for."

Sheila started the gas stove and soon had a warm cup of tea and was heating one of her instant dinners. "If I knew where you were camping, I would come over and ask for a cup of coffee," she smiled, feeling deliciously wicked.

"I bet I could seduce you," she said, feeling her skin warm with her thought. "I bet you would like me."

She laughed—picturing him naked. He would have a deeply sunburned face and hands, while the rest of his body would be as pale as snow. His face would be creased like old paper from squinting at the sun and his hands would be calloused and hard and covered with small nicks.

She thought about her husband, his hands had been soft, his touches always tentative. But his touches had thrilled her, not so much from his passion but because she loved him so, and gave herself to him, released in her giving.

She pictured her legs wrapped around the cowboy's back as he arched on top of her—her breasts smashed by his weight as they made love on the edge of a clearing with two horse blankets as their bed. She could smell the sweat of the horses mixed with the odor of the man, a strange, mystifying odor. An odor mixed with the outdoors—clear streams, stars, thrashing storms.

"Why didn't you wave back?" she demanded. "I know you saw me."

Sheila ate her food and sipped the tea. She heard a creature moving through the trees but was not afraid. Small clouds drifted over the half moon, blocking out the moon shadow of the large spruce tree. She caught the darting glimmer of a shooting star. She thought of the city and how she never saw the night sky. There was no night sky, the star beams were washed away by city lights, as if by light man could drive away his fear of the darkness—or—his fear of himself.

Sheila made another cup of tea and went inside the tent. She liked how the faint glow of the candle lantern filled the tent. It was like the inside of an empty church. She was a part of a stained glass window. Only, her window was a small glow on the side of the mountain. The glow called out. I live, I am, remember me.

Feeling restless, Sheila went back outside. "I wonder if I can see his camp?"

She gazed at all the gray outlines of hills but could see no lantern light or flickering fire flame. "If you were here I would keep you warm tonight," she said. "If you were here I would rub your back."

She stood silently for a few minutes, went back inside the tent and finished her tea. She removed all her clothes, wondering and hoping he could see her camp and see her naked form through the tent. She got into the sleeping bag, the cold fabric making goose bumps all over her body. "If you were here you could hold me," she said quietly. "You could even sleep alone and I could listen to you breathe and wonder what you are dreaming. You could leave in the morning if you wanted, as long as you smiled and promised to wave the next time you saw me."

Sheila blew out the candle. There was nothing in the darkness, no warmth, no cold. There was nothing in the silence. "I would have liked to have met you, really I would. I would have liked to have spent an evening listening to your stories and finding out about your life."

Shutting her eyes the fact he had not waved made her sad. She was a lover who had been abandoned—but—even in her abandonment—the thought of him drove a small amount of the loneliness away.

The Mountain
Once There Was A Hermit

It seems all mountains at one time or another have had a hermit. Most hermits are called crazy, or insane, but maybe they are sane in their craziness. One day something in their mind tells them enough is enough and they leave everything behind and head out to some far corner of the earth where they can be alone.

Nobody really remembers when the hermit moved to the mountain. The people in town and the ranchers did not know much about him or really cared. They had their hands full trying to make ends meet. They did have one common opinion though; it was the hermit's right to be whatever he wanted to be and if he did not want to be bothered than leave the poor bastard alone.

This hermit was a smart hermit—if there is such a thing as a dumb hermit—he claimed a parcel of land for a mining claim, which cost him very little every year, as long as he could prove he was looking for gold or silver. He did this by digging a hole once a year on his claim.

With nothing but a handsaw and an axe, he built a one room cabin and his furniture, hauled in the rest of what he needed with his horse and settled in for a peaceful life. If he was crazy, he would not get lonely. If he was not crazy, he got used to being lonely.

After several years, the hermit rode his horse into town, rented a Post Office box, and sent an ad to Outdoor Life advertising to guide hunters, fishermen, or people who wanted to take photographs of the mountains. His ad also stated he had no phone and all interested parties needed to reply by a given date so he could write them and tell them where to meet him. When he came into town to buy a few supplies and check his mail he never said more than a few words to anybody, usually a vague "yep," or "nope."

There is really no need to be a hermit if you are going to talk all the time.

Within a few years, he had several hunters and fishermen that came to hunt and fish each year. They stayed in his cabin and since most of the hunters were trophy hunters, he got to keep the meat and they took the head. The money they paid him was enough for his simple needs for the upcoming year. When his clients were in town, they never talked about the hermit, as though one of the hermit's conditions to guide them was they could not tell people about him.

Everything went along fine for years until one-summer three rich men from back east, exploring the high country for good trout fishing, discovered an old abandoned mining town located on the side of the mountain. The road that led into it had long ago washed out and rutted and very few people ever went to the town. The three men bought the town and over the next several years built a small hotel and a restaurant and had the road graded and graveled. It was their plan to hire cowboys to lead people back into the wilderness on one and two day rides. They did not expect to make a lot of money, which did not matter, they had a lot of money. All three were driven by their love of the mountains and the desire for people to see the high country. It also provided jobs for cowboys who were finding it hard to find work and more and more were ending up driving trucks or being bartenders. A sad lot for a cowboy.

When the town was renovated and people started taking the pack trips the hermit's life began changing. Now, instead of a few people being in the mountains during the summer and fall, the mountain was becoming a regular circus. The trails were littered with candy bar wrappers, cigarette butts and horse manure. Sitting in his cabin at night, the hermit could hear people playing guitars and singing and when he was on his porch, he could see distant camp fires. When he went to the lakes to fish, there was always a group of people wearing expensive waders, staying in wall tents and fishing only with flies. They eyed him suspiciously like he was some kind of alien.

The hermit suffered in silence for the first couple of years. He picked up candy bar wrappers and cigarette butts and only went fishing when the weather was bad—knowing he would not see anybody else. He contemplated building a fence around his claim, but the idea of fencing his claim made him feel like he would be fencing himself in rather than fencing others out.

After another year, the hermit had about all he could stand of people on his mountain and began fighting back. When people were not around he tore down their tents and scattered the gear.

It was during this time, the government, seeing into the future, designated mountains all over the country as wilderness areas, meaning they could not be mined, lumbered, or anything else that might destroy their beauty. Also, no motorized vehicles could enter them, no chain saws, or anything mechanical. Plus, access could only be by foot or horseback. These lands were called lands of the people. But, ranchers, with their strong Washington lobby, made it possible to lease grazing rights in the wilderness areas for their cattle and sheep. This was good for the ranchers—they got cheap feed, but bad for the mountain—trails started to erode away from cattle tromping on them and portions of streams and beaver ponds turned into cesspools of cow manure. Neither the cattle nor the cowboys who checked on them bothered the hermit, but now that the land was 'the people's land' there had to be 'the people's police' or, a game warden to patrol the mountain.

The game warden that was assigned to the mountain was not a bad guy. He let the locals poach a few deer and rarely checked a local for a fishing or hunting license. When it came to out-of-state fishermen and hunters, he checked their licenses like they were mass murderers. One day, with nothing important to do, he rode his mule to visit the hermit. "Nice place," he said to the hermit, who was splitting wood outside his cabin.

"Yep," the hermit replied.

"How's the fishing?" the warden asked.

"Good," the hermit replied.

The warden knew the hermit did not have a fishing license or a hunting license or the now required guiding permit.

"You need help, you know where I am," the warden said.

"Nice mule," the hermit said.

As the warden rode off the mountain he thought to himself, "I like the old geezer."

When the small acts of sabotage started, the warden knew who was doing it and one afternoon he rode back to the hermit's cabin. The warden did not get off his mule when he said, "You have to stop destroying people's property."

The hermit did not reply.

"I know how you feel, but times change," the warden said.

The hermit still did not reply.

"People have to see these mountains," the warden continued, "People have forgotten where they came from, people have to get out and touch the sky and see the trees. They have to wonder. Life has no wonder in it anymore."

The hermit still did not reply.

The warden smiled thinly, "I don't want to have to come in and pack you off to jail."

He started to turn his mule to leave. "You like some coffee?" the hermit asked.

The warden tried not to act surprised as he dismounted and tied his mule to a hitching post in front of the cabin.

The cabin was clean inside. The handmade chairs and tables were covered with crude carved figures of birds and animals. Candles were scattered around the room. A Mason canning jar was setting in the middle of the dinning table with flowers in it. Hanging on the wall were two framed photographs of the hermit as a younger man with his arm around a woman. A cross made from cedar was nailed on the wall over a bed. As the hermit heated coffee on a tin sheepherder's wood stove, he did not speak. Setting the coffee cups down he sat across from the warden. The warden felt uneasy as he sipped his coffee.

The hermit pursed his lips, and looked directly in the warden's eyes. "I'm afraid," he said. "The mountain is dying."

"You can't stop it, you know that," the warden replied.

"Yep," the hermit said, and said no more.

The two men sat in silence until the coffee was finished.

As the warden rode his mule off the mountain he saw the candy bar wrappers, the gum wrappers, the cigarette butts and all the tracks from boots and sneakers and they seemed to shout at him.

After the warden's visit to the hermit, there was no more vandalism of camps and no sightings of the hermit. No hunters or fishermen come through town to fish and hunt with the hermit that fall.

After winter set in, and before the snow grew too deep, the warden decided to ride to the hermit's house and check on him. When he got to the cabin there was no sign of life, no stacked wood, no horse in the corral, no smoke curling from the stovepipe. The warden called out but there was no reply. Fearing the worst, he apprehensively went inside the cabin. The cabin had not been lived in for a long time. The two photographs were the only things missing from the cabin.

Eating breakfast the next morning at the cafe all the locals wanted to know if he had seen the hermit. Looking out the window toward the mountain he told the men in a dry, far away voice, "There's no room for a hermit in this world anymore," and after a pause, added, "He couldn't watch the dying."

The Man
The Present

Bill knew it would only take him another hour to get to the meadow and the bones. From the meadow, the mountains stretched out into the distance as far as the eye could see. "I could ride forever and never reach the end," she said in awe.

Bill got down from the horse and started unpacking his gear. Gypsy looked at him strangely and snapped at a bothersome sweat bee. Bill did not pitch the tent but built a lean-to.

They had stopped early in the morning. Bill wanting to go on but she wanted to stop. Bill always did what she wanted. It did not make him feel less than a man to make her smile. It was a day like today—warm and sunny, everything seemingly at peace with the world—except the flies and sweat bees. "I can see why you love it so up here," she said. "I always wondered how a man could love riding around the mountains, getting rained on and snowed on, bit by bugs, but I can understand now."

The statement made Bill feel odd. Not in a way that bothered him but in a way that perplexed him. He always thought when one fell in love, the person who returned the love automatically knew their partner—knew everything. But, Bill was surprised when he discovered she really did not know him like he thought she did. She really did not know anything about him. But, after awhile, he knew there was nothing he could do about it. It was a not-so-good fact of life.

"This is like a fantasyland," she said. "It's like nothing else in the world is real. What we all spend our lives doing is erased as soon as we get in the mountains."

"If we lived in the mountains than this would be the reality and the city would be a fantasy," he said.

"If the mountains had breasts you wouldn't need me," she said with her teasing look.

He remembered trying to say something to let her know how much he loved her but had only fumbled out some words that made no sense. He always felt he made no sense when he talked to her. He was like a little boy trying to lie to his mother and the more he lied, the more far fetched the lie became. After a few moments of silence he told her, "I love you."

"I know," she said. "But you love the mountains more."

Bill did not reply. In many ways he supposed he did. He was at ease in the mountains. But, when he was in the mountains and away from her, he missed her. Maybe all love was, was missing someone.

"At least you love the mountains and not some bargirl in one of those awful towns we drove through," she said.

Bill smiled at her and thought about some of the bargirls scattered throughout his life and felt sad—sad for the girls and sad for himself. Sad that he had only used them, a list of girls with empty eyes and no names, shadows moving through a world of smoke and liquor.

Building a fire Bill set the water-filled coffeepot in the middle of it. Gypsy lay in the shade of a tree ignoring the cloud of mosquitoes swirling around her head. When the water was hot, Bill put in a handful of coffee.

"You want to what?" she said.

"Let's make love in the trees," he repeated.

"You feel seventeen?" she asked.

Bill knew she was not excited about his invitation.

"Okay," she said.

She was beautiful lying naked on the ground surrounded by the wind and the forest. The white of her skin was like a fresh patch of snow. He always felt she was too pretty for him. Too soft and too smart. "I like my men ugly," she laughed when he brought up the subject. "Ugly and dumb. Then I can get away with more."

The idea of making love seemed romantic, but the mosquito bites were not. Bill sipped his coffee and for a moment smiled, remembering the mosquito bites all over their bodies.

She was at work when he brought the horse home and put her in the end stall, making sure she would not see it when she came home. It was her birthday and he was excited with his gift.

He did not mention her birthday while they ate dinner and he knew by her actions she thought he had forgotten. "I need your help in the barn," he said after she had done the dishes.

She had followed him to the barn without speaking. "Go get that shovel in the last stall," he told her.

The horse neighed when she opened the door—a big red bow was tied to its forelock and a sign hung around its neck—'Happy Birthday.'

She kissed him, and hugged him, and cried. "She is so pretty."

Only after she stopped crying did she punch him in the stomach. "You bastard," she said.

The punch was hard enough to hurt but Bill only laughed.

The horse was a bay quarter horse mare, gentle as spring, with a red tint to her hair. Her mane and tail were long and her eyes were patient. "I'm going to call her Texas Lady," she said, adding, "you're not going to take her to the mountains either, so don't even ask."

The horse turned out to be one of the best horses Bill had ever been around. She was gentle, but still filled with spirit. She rode Texas Lady into the mountains with him. Bill had never loved horses—but she loved that horse.

Gypsy came back covered with mud. So many mosquitoes had bitten the tips of her ears they were bleeding but, when Bill tried to touch them, she moved her head and yelped. "You big baby," Bill said.

"Only people who love you miss you," Bill said to the dog. "Nobody else really cares."

Gypsy looked at him distantly with her deep topaz eyes. "All you want is food, you lousy old dog," Bill said.

The dog's tail thumped on the ground. "I bet she would have found somebody else by now," Bill said. "She would have gone on with her life."

Bill rummaged through the packs while Gypsy eagerly watched. He got out two patties of dry, chewy dog food and slowly unwrapped them, teasing the dog. He set them on the ground. Gypsy did not go to them until he headed toward the horses.

The horses were covered with mosquitoes and when Bill ran his hand along their sides, his hand came away covered with blood. The mosquitoes would go away when the sun began to go down. The dropping temperature of the high country would drive them into the trees for the night.

When Bill got back to the camp, Gypsy had finished the food and sat looking at him like she was bored. Bill poured himself another cup of coffee. He knew he should eat something but he did not feel hungry. His stomach held all his tension in a ball as tight as a fist. "She would like me to find somebody," he said to Gypsy. "If somebody loves you, they want you to be happy, or at least not be alone."

Finishing his coffee Bill gathered wood for the night. He knew he would not sleep. He was too close to the ghosts to sleep, too close to the bones. For over an hour he gathered wood, far more than he would need, but, he felt satisfaction in knowing somebody would use it one day. There was something comforting about coming across an abandoned camp in the mountains with a stack of wood. "I leave you a gift of fire," he thought.

He understood how primitive man could worship fire. Man sitting and looking at a fire did not think about being alone—the flame was a gift of life.

When it was dark, Bill built up the fire. He lay a horse blanket on the ground for Gypsy to lie on. It was a pretty night. There was no wind and cool enough the bugs were gone. Bill was struck by the thought he had seen little sign of deer and elk during his ride. It would be a bad year for hunters.

Bill got a can of tuna out of the pack. He opened the can and ate the tuna without crackers. The tuna seemed foreign. He could see images of the great fish as they were dragged into the boat, thrashing in the nets and gasping for breath. He wondered if fish cried when they were clubbed to death while they flopped on the slippery decks of the fishing boat. He wondered if some fish were smart like the old and wise deer and elk that hid from hunters. Bill tossed the can in the fire and watched as the fire burnt the paper wrapper from the can.

The tuna made him feel better and he poured himself another cup of coffee. A slight breeze kicked up and one of the horses neighed—the sound carrying for miles on the wind. Gypsy was asleep, her side moving in and out slowly, peacefully.

"The world doesn't go away when you're up here," she said. "When you ride off it's all still the same."

He wanted to tell her this was his world. A world devoid of people, harsh enough in its own right, but still devoid of people. He wanted to tell her he could not make any sense out of life but she made it easier. Why? He did not know?

She was sleeping by a log one afternoon. Bill watched her while she slept—the small lines by her eyes, and the way her eyelids fluttered. He felt closer to her than when she was awake. Her sleeping was telling him, "I trust you."

Bill tossed the remaining coffee into the fire. "I will touch the bones and make a shrine of them," he said. "I will touch the bones and when I do, I will go on with my life."

Gypsy's feet started moving and she whimpered in her sleep. Bill got his heavier coat from the pack and put it on. Sitting in his lean-to he gazed into the fire. He hoped the night passed quickly. A log popped, sending a shower of sparks into the air. The sparks cascading back toward the ground like tiny glowing lives falling into the darkness. "I should have waved at the lady," Bill muttered. "She might have needed a wave."

The Woman
Mushrooms

According to Sheila's map, the meadow that was her destination was only a few hours away. She was both happy and sad. Happy in knowing she would reach her destination and sad in knowing once she did, she would turn around and head back to the real world. "For a city girl you did damn good," she told herself. "Damn good."

After hiking for the past days, there was a spring in Sheila's step and she was vibrantly alive. The sun had turned her legs, arms, and face, a deep brown, while her nose was a pale red. She wished once again she had gone camping with her husband and wondered what it was that had made her feel having her own identity was so important. "Lord, what we sacrifice in the name of self," she mused.

Sheila put the map away and swung the pack easily onto her back. She had not gone more than a hundred yards when she saw them. Growing in an area not more than ten yards square, on a pine shaded bank, were enough golden chanterelle mushrooms for an army. The golden caps were like a cluster of yellow butterflies drying their wings after a summer rain. Not more than twenty feet from the mushrooms was a sunshine filled clearing. The ground was covered with a deep carpet of pine needles. Feeling like a young girl about to go on her first date, she made her camp, expecting to see a leprechaun stick his head up from behind a rock at any moment.

When her camp was set and she had gathered enough wood for her evening fire she took a plastic bag and walked to the mushroom patch, thinking about all the fancy dans sitting in expensive restaurants eating chanterelles. She carefully cut the mushroom stems at ground level, not wanting to disturb the spore. After she had cut about a pound, she went back to camp feeling more contentment in her heart than she had felt in years. She hummed an old song as she washed the mushrooms. A quick thought crossed her mind of driving down the freeway with her husband while the same song played on the radio, but it did not make her feel sad or alone.

Sheila cooked the mushrooms over her stove and feeling decadent wished she had a bottle of white wine. Thinking about the wine, she laughed. "I wonder what that cowboy would say if he came across me eating mushrooms and drinking white wine in the wilderness?"

It seemed ludicrous, but sinfully delightful.

She had a naughty vision of walking into the cowboy's camp wearing a black teddy and black hose and carrying a silver tray with a platter of mushrooms, a bottle of wine and two wine glasses. She giggled, "better than campfire coffee you no waving cowboy."

Sheila ate the mushrooms with her fingers. They had an earthy nutty taste and were delicious. When she finished, she made herself a cup of tea. Sipping her tea she contemplated how, in literature, it always said, "The silence of the forest."

The forest was anything but silent—filled with the creaks and groans of swaying trees, the tapping of woodpeckers, the shrill cries of mountain jays and the haunting screeches of hunting hawks. The forest was a chorus of sounds. She wondered how her life would have been different if she would have been raised a country girl. Would she have rebelled and run to the city? Not seeing the beauty in the world that had been around her.

She tossed out the remaining tea and decided to go for a walk. After a few steps she turned and looking back at her camp she felt proud. After walking for a few more minutes, she started talking. "You would have liked the mushrooms."

She did not feel sad but slightly empty, as though a part of her had floated away into the sky. "We could have eaten and then you would have taken me into the tent."

Sheila smiled, thinking about when they were first married and had taken a vow to make love on all the different pieces of furniture in the house, even standing in the kitchen sink. She wondered if her parents had ever made love in the kitchen sink. Thinking about it, she doubted it, but she hoped they had.

She stopped and examined moss clinging to the side of a tree. She ran her hands over the moss. She had the feeling that even the moss, in its own way could think, and could realize it was alive. Turning, she headed back toward her camp.

She wondered what the cowboy was doing? "I bet if I would have stood up on that rock and taken off my shirt and waved at you, you would have waved back."

She wondered if he would call her ma'am. She could see him, tall and tough, with his hat in his hand stammering, "Yes ma'am, no ma'am."

Back at her camp she was touched once more by its beauty. The tent was like a blue mushroom growing from the earth. She waited until the sun started going down before starting a fire. As the fire caught, it seemed as though it was a life—it could dream and hope, it could dance.

It was a beautiful night and the stars shone through the canopy of trees and Sheila wondered what people were doing back in the city. "I don't even know what is going on in the world now," she said. "There might be a war, the President might be dead, California might have fallen into the ocean."

None of those things seemed to matter or to have any bearing on her life.

Sheila heard a horse neigh in the distance and the sound of the horse filled her with longing. There was no doubt in her mind the horse belonged to the cowboy. She could picture him sitting by a fire, drinking coffee from a tin cup. His hat would be pushed back on his head and the dog would be lying by his leg. He was covered by the same stars she was seeing, feeling the same wind, hearing the same sounds. She wanted to stand and call to him, wondering if he would call back? But she did not.

The horse neighed once again and she envisioned the cowboy getting up and walking into the darkness to check on his horses. Maybe there was a wolf, or a mountain lion. Strangely, the thought did not scare her.

Sheila did not move for several hours. Her mind absorbed by the fire and the night, and thoughts of the cowboy. She went into the tent and sat on her sleeping bag for a few minutes listening to the wind rustle against the nylon. She thought of her doors at home with their chain locks and dead bolts. Lying in her sleeping bag, she wondered if the cowboy would be gentle if he made love to her? She could feel his arm slide over her body and hold her. Sitting up, she peered into the darkness. Taking a deep breath, she started to call out, but stopped, and lay back down, alone, and searching for a dream.

The Mountain
Only The Blind Can See

At one time there was a silver mine on the mountain. Not one of those famous glory holes that made the newspaper headlines back east and men scurried to in hordes with dreams of quick riches, but it was large enough that, for a short while, it gave many people in the area jobs. It also attracted gamblers, prostitutes, and the various other vagabonds that went from mining town to mining town hoping to reap the rewards of other men's toil.

Mr. Jacop Smith fancied himself a card shark. His trade served him well for many years. Although not the best card shark in the world, he had enough sense to stay away from the real fancy towns and preyed on the, as he called them, "less favorable pickings."

Jacop Smith was fifty years old, not a handsome man, rather short and round, with long bushy sideburns and a red glow to his puffy face. He resembled a preacher more than a gambler. But, hidden behind the mirth-filled blue eyes and smiling lips was the heart of a man who only thought about himself.

When the mine on the mountain was doing well, Mr. Smith came riding into town with a lady thirty years his junior. Unlike Jacop, the lady was small, seemingly frail, with a sallow complexion and a tight composure to her face as if all feeling had been beaten out of her. She was raised in a sod house in Kansas by a father who should have been killed for how he treated his family. She was sixteen when she ran off and made her way to Denver. In Denver she called herself Penny Rose and took a job in a house of ill repute. Although not pretty, she got a steady patronage of mostly older men and, unlike most ladies of her trade, she did not spend her money on fancy clothes but saved every cent she could in a cherrywood box covered with hand-carved dragons. The elderly patron who gave her the box telling her it had come all the way from China. The key to the box hung securely around her neck from a blue ribbon.

Sitting in her room in the early mornings, with the cherrywood box of money in her lap, Penny Rose would dream about San Francisco and how one day she would live by the ocean and have lace curtains on her windows that would not shut out the light. In her mind, she could see the gulls and smell the ocean.

Mr. Jacop Smith arrived in Denver with little more than his wagon, having found out Santa Fe was not a good town for small time hustlers. Caught trying to feed himself an ace, he was almost hanged, but managed to buy his way out of the mess with his gold watch and his diamond pinky ring. After selling his horse and wagon in Denver, he managed to win some money and half drunk, he fell into the arms of Penny Rose. In his usual, jovial manner, he told her he was on his way to San Francisco. As things go in the world, Penny dug out her cherrywood dragon-covered box from underneath her bed and told Mr. Jacop Smith she would help finance the trip if only he would take her with him. Having been a prostitute for three years, she was more than well versed in the ways of men, but the slim chance of realizing her dream was far more powerful than common sense.

What started out as the journey to the land of dreams soon turned into a journey from one mining town to another. Jacop saying all the time, "Just one more town my dear, just one more town and we'll go to San Francisco."

All the while, the money going into the cherrywood dragon-covered box was far less than the money coming out.

When Jacop and Penny arrived at the mining town on the mountain, Penny had all but given up her dream and was falling into a deep depression. A depression she did not show by anger or crosswords but with a lifeless, dull look in her eyes. Much like the look she had used as a small girl to stop her father from beating her. To Penny, the town was like all the other towns, with its piles of slag and mud streets lined with tents and rough buildings identified with crudely, scrawled signs.

Jacop rented a room and as usual spent all his time in the bars plying his trade. Penny was contemplating taking the little remaining money and returning to Denver when she discovered she was pregnant. Within several weeks a transformation came over her. A rosy tint spread over her complexion and her gaunt features rounded off to soft curves giving her an almost beautiful appearance. Her eyes lit up like a small girl with a secret. She started to knit, even at times singing in her high frail voice.

The night she told Jacop she was pregnant, he, in his normal jolly way, expounded the merits of children and promised her they would soon leave for the coast, as a child should not be raised in mining camps. But that night as Penny slept, he cut the blue ribbon with the key from around her neck and taking the remaining money out of the cherrywood dragon-covered box he stole from town.

When Penny woke in the morning, she saw the blue ribbon with the key lying on the dresser. Frantically grabbing the key she opened the box, finding the box empty, she crumpled, sobbing, to the floor.

For two days Penny sat by the window and gazed listlessly over the ugly town. When it grew dark on the second day, she removed her clothes, picked up one of her knitting needles and was about to insert it into her uterus when there was a knock on the door. At first she ignored the knock but when it persisted, she dressed and answered the door. A tall, slender man with only one arm and deep, dark, sad eyes removed his hat when she opened the door. "I'm Tim Powers," he said in a voice that barely penetrated Penny's mind. "I heard about your husband and I came to ask you if you would move into my house."

Penny motioned for him to come into the room. Sitting on the bed, she bowed her head and began to cry. Great tears streamed down her face while her shoulders heaved with her sobs. Mr. Powers let her cry and then packed her few belongings, including the cherrywood box, took her hand and gently led her out of the rooming house to the edge of town where he had built a four-room log cabin.

He showed her to her own room and made it clear she was not obligated to him in anyway.

Mr. Powers was a quiet, unlearned man. His arm was torn off working the mine and with the loss of his arm, he forever gave up the thought of striking it rich. He ran a laundry and the stable, both of which made him enough money to be comfortable. The first time he saw Penny Rose as she was riding into town he fell in love with her.

It took five months for Penny Rose to come out of her depression.

During those months, she did not cook, and rarely left her room. Tim brought her food and talked to her as one would talk to a child.

It was a sunny fall day. The mountain was cloaked in deep shades of yellow and red when Penny Rose returned to the world. She was sitting in her room when the baby kicked. Later, when Tim came into her room with her supper, she was holding her stomach and smiled at him.

The next day when Tim came back from the livery, the house had been cleaned and Penny had made dinner. While eating, Tim said. "It is a good home for a child."

That night Penny moved into Tim's room. They lay in bed and Tim holding her in his arms listened to the two heartbeats pulsing within her.

The room Penny had lived in was turned into a baby's room. Tim built a crib and installed a small wood stove. When Penny went into labor, a German lady who did not speak good English delivered the baby. It was an easy birth and the round, baby girl was healthy and rosy in color, but she was born with no eyes. Her sunken eye sockets lay veiled with a sheet of pale skin. The German lady said to Tim in her heavy accent, "Vee all have a purpose," and went home to her six children.

They named the baby Rebecca and showered her dark world with sunshine. When Tim left in the mornings to go to work, Penny would hold Rebecca in her arms and sit by the window. As the baby suckled at her breast she would look out the window at the mountains, but dreaming about San Francisco, she would say, "There on the horizon I can see the sail of a mighty ship. Around her mast, gulls with their gray and black wings beg for food. On the dock there is a man selling crabs and soon the tide will come in...."

When Tim came home at night, his dinner would be prepared and the house clean. But he knew Penny had a great longing in her heart, a longing he could never touch, nor bear to ask about. He never asked the story behind the cherrywood box that sat on the dresser in their room.

As the child grew the mine diminished, as if each year of growth indicated decline. The town began to dry up and the prostitutes, gamblers, and miners went off chasing other dreams. Tim remained, barely making a living but feeding Penny and her daughter. Penny knew Tim loved her but, although cooking his meals and warming his bed, she remained a stranger.

As the child grew in her dark world, Penny and Tim realized Rebecca was also simple. She could do little more than grunt or wail and roll her head on her shoulders like a ship drifting on a rolling sea. Tim still loved the child, "The simple are the true teachers," he told Penny. "God has blessed them with no malice in their hearts."

And still Penny would sit by the window and talk to the child. "I can see the fleet coming in with its day's catch of flounder and crabs. I can see the tall waves roll in and touch the beach and the men who collect seashells to make trinkets for the tourists...."

Rebecca would sit, seeing nothing, rolling her head from side to side, listening intently to the soft voice of her mother.

When Rebecca was eleven, the mine closed and Tim moved Penny and Rebecca to a small town not far from the mountain. As they rode in the wagon with all their possessions, Penny imagined she was on her way to San Francisco. She had never told Tim about her dream of San Francisco—she held it in her heart like a prayer candle lighting up her night.

The town was a quiet place with a dry good store, a newspaper, a school and three churches. Tim got a job as a clerk at the store.

Now Penny would sit with Rebecca and look at the mountain and tell her, "One day I will take you to the beach, you will feel the ocean on your feet, I will put salt water on your lips and you will laugh...."

When Rebecca was seventeen, Tim died suddenly at work. The preacher came to the door and Penny listened to the dreadful words. It was as if all the years she had been with Tim came down upon her like an early snowfall in the mountains. Crumbling to her knees she realized how kind Tim had been to her and how she had really loved him but never told him.

After Tim was buried, a smartly dressed lawyer arrived on the train from Denver, and gave Penny Rose a check for twenty two thousand dollars and a letter written by Tim. "I want you to know I loved you. There is nothing more I can say. Put this in your cherrywood dream box."

After the lawyer left, Penny Rose sat in the kitchen for many hours gazing at the check through tear-filled eyes. Four days later she and Rebecca were on the train for San Francisco. The first day on the train, she threw the cherrywood dragon-covered box out the window.

In San Francisco, she bought a small house overlooking the ocean. She put lace curtains on the windows. From her living room she could smell the sea and hear the gulls and watch the fishing boats come in with the tide. In the early evenings, she would put Rebecca in a chair facing out the window, sit beside her and tell her, "The mountain is tall, you can see bands of dark green scrub oak winding like rivers at its base, down one side aspen groves whisper with the wind, and a clear stream feeds beaver ponds where brook trout dart through the crystal clear water and jump for small scurrying bugs. The top of the mountain is covered with snow and the meadows dotting its sides are filled with wildflowers of all colors...."

Rebecca would sit, her head rolling from side to side, listening to her mother's soft words and be content.

The Man
The Shrine

Bill was shaving. He had a metal mirror wedged between a tree limb and the trunk. Wiping off the remaining soap, he examined his image in the scratched mirror. It seemed like a weight was pulling his eyelids down, as though life did not want him to see, or feel, and it was only with great effort that he kept his gray eyes open. His handlebar moustache, which he was always proud of, offended him. His lips were not frowning but also not smiling—as if any sign of emotion was bad. When he was younger, he always set his jaw so he looked tough, but now he did not want to look tough—he wanted to smile—like with her.

He thought about a story he had heard on the radio about a man whose son was stabbed ten times before the attacker killed him. When the killer was about to be electrocuted, the father told him, "I forgive you."

"He's a stronger man than I am," Bill muttered.

Bill put the mirror in his shaving kit and methodically packed up the gear. Gypsy was on a hillside trying to catch a rock chuck. Her barks another sound of the forest. When the horses were packed, Bill pulled himself up into the saddle like an old man whose bones and muscles were forsaking him. It would not take him long to get to the meadow. A gut wrenching fear swept through him. The same shattering fear that came over him as a young man before he boarded the helicopter—a fear that bound men to war, each wanting to run, but unable to let their comrades think they might be a coward.

Taking several deep breaths Bill nudged the horse with his boot heels trying to forget that day. Everything he saw now, she had seen, every tree, every stand of flowers, every moss-covered rock. She had seen it all, she had shared it with him—excited, smiling, free, happy.

Gypsy ran by the feet of the horse, the bell packed with mud and not jingling. The horse tried to kick Gypsy—she dodged it with the nonchalance of a boxer fighting a man he knew he would beat.

Bill sagged in the saddle. He thought about all the death he had seen, but it had been death for a cause, a reason, a purpose to die. Her death had no reason, no purpose—random death. Why would an almighty God look down and say you will be killed for no reason? You will be smiling and happy and you will die. "Maybe it is a blessing to die when you least expect it?" he said. "To die with a smile on your face and be killed so quickly death cannot be recognized or feared."

Bill straightened up in the saddle. "Ever since I figured out there is no reason to anything, it's been better," he said. But then he thought, "There has to be a reason, having no reason has left me lifeless."

The trail made a slight curve and then turned into a long series of switchbacks that zigzagged up a pine tree covered hillside. The trail ran beside a tumbling stream that began its life in the patches of frozen snow above timberline.

Riding up the trail Bill stared down at the ground trying to shut out any sight they would have seen together, as if not seeing would erase the photographs of that day from his mind. But, it did not help, he could hear her joyful words. "Did you see that bird? Did you hear that sound? It smells so fresh, so lovely."

Bill sighed and rubbed his forehead, thinking about the first time he came to the meadow. He was scouting for elk for a client who only wanted a record elk so Bill had gone on his search, riding into the canyons and corners of the wilderness where the big bulls would hide knowing they were the grand prize. In the late fall he found the elk, a nice royal. In October, when the hunter came, an early snowfall covered the meadow with three feet of snow, but still they forced their way to it. After hours of back breaking work, all they found in the meadow was a furrow the large elk's stomach had left in the snow as he headed into a canyon so steep they could not follow. To Bill's relief, the hunter only laughed and they fought their way down the mountain, passing up shots on many smaller elk as they descended. The hunter tipped Bill five hundred dollars and sent him a Christmas card each year—the last one telling Bill he had stopped hunting and taken up photographing trophy class animals with a camera mounted on a rifle stock.

Bill was no more than three hundred yards from the meadow when he came to the stream. They had stopped here. "I would have liked to crawl into your eyes once," Bill said, remembering how she had marveled at the tiny crystalline rainbows that shimmered in the mist over the tumbling stream.

"I would have liked to have seen your world for only a few minutes," Bill said.

Bill grew cold and buttoned the top button of his shirt. "God, I hope you know how much I loved you," he said, almost trembling.

With a vengeance he kicked the horse, jolting her from her rest. The packhorse's neck was stretched out by the sudden jerk on the lead rope and it faltered before being yanked into a trot. When they bolted into the meadow, Bill kicked the horse again, forcing her to go faster, tearing through the meadow like a mad man, grim-faced, until they reached the other side where he yanked back on the reins causing the two horses to skid to a stop. Gypsy ran around the horses and barked several times, sensing the urgency, but not seeing any danger.

Bill dismounted quickly and unpacked the horses, throwing the gear to the ground. He long-lined the horses to trees where there was plenty of grass and started pitching his tent like a man who would drop dead if the tent was not pitched. Gypsy, with her ears laid back, watched Bill as if he were a stranger, someone she did not know enough to trust.

When the tent was pitched, Bill gathered wood. Running around like a demon, bringing in arm loads of wood, enough wood for a week. When the wood lay in a heap, he dug out a fire pit and scoured the meadow for rocks to surround it. He was sweating and his breath came in shallow, raspy bursts. He stacked a pile of wood, squirted kerosene on it and struck a match. As he was about to light the logs, he pulled his hand back slowly and blew out the match. Gypsy crept up to him like she was afraid he would lash out and strike her, something he had never done. She tentatively nuzzled his hand with her cold nose but Bill did not respond. Bill was glaring at the charred, shattered tops of several trees where lightning had struck. He went over to a tree and sat down with his back resting against the trunk. Gypsy lay down by his extended legs, the warmth of her body oblivious to Bill.

"It hasn't changed," Bill said, his voice sounding far away as if the years would have changed the meadow, erased it from being, making the reality of what had happened only a bad dream.

He saw their old camp—the pile of rotting wood and the circle of rocks for a fire. He knew the ridgepoles for the tent were in the trees along with the grill. The old camp was a nightmare that would never go away—even when the firewood was long rotted to dust and the rocks for the fire so overgrown they could not be seen.

Bill closed his eyes. The day had dawned quiet and peaceful with a slight hint of dew on the grass. While they drank coffee, her face seemed to swim in a circle of gold, and in the circle, her features were clear—it was as though he had never really seen her before. When she noticed him gazing at her, she gave him a puzzled look, smiled, and said nothing.

By the time they finished breakfast the day was changing, a cold wind blew in, whipping the trees. "Let's pack up," he told her, "this could blow in a bad one."

"We can sit in the tent," she said, smiling, looking free and wild as the wind tossed her hair. "Besides, we haven't made love in eight hours."

Bill remembered looking at the darkening sky and then back at her and forgetting the storm, following her into the tent.

The storm exploded with thunderclaps that jolted the ground like earthquake aftershocks. Gypsy rushed into the tent and lay shaking by the flap. Flashes of lightning filled the air with electricity, scorching molecules of oxygen in its wrath and leaving the air smelling like gunpowder. The first blast woke Bill from her naked breasts and he was afraid. He had never been afraid in a storm and it perplexed him. Storms were part of the mystery, part of the make-up of a man who made his living away from the soft parts of the world.

"You can see why Indians worshipped lightning," she said, rubbing her hands on his bare back. "It's a god of anger and fear."

She started to dress. Bill was not really watching her as he listened to the storm, wondering why he was afraid. It was only when she was at the tent flap and about to go outside that he realized what she was doing. "Don't go out," he ordered.

"I want to be with the storm," she said, leaving the tent.

Bill scrambled out of the sleeping bag and dressed as quickly as he could. Gypsy still cowered by the tent flap as the thunderclaps boomed and the streaks of lightning increased in intensity. Bill had just put his boots on when the rain came like thousands of machine guns mowing down an advancing army. It was so thick and heavy he could not see more than three feet past the flap of the tent. As quickly as the rain burst started, it slowed, as if a giant hand had turned off a switch. A fine drizzle fell and the lightning stopped. The sky, which had been dark, turned an eerie grayish white. Bill felt relieved as he left the tent—Gypsy still cowering by the flap.

He saw her by the edge of the meadow, she was patting the neck of Texas Lady, her soaked hair hanging straight down her back and her cloths clinging to her like a multi-colored layer of skin. Seeing Bill she waved. Her smile flew across the meadow like a songbird's melody and Bill waved back, feeling more in love than he ever had in his life. Gypsy came out of the tent and ran to her in a playful bouncy pattern. When Gypsy reached her, she bent over and lovingly patted the dog and started leading Texas Lady toward the tent. Gypsy ran and barked towards Bill.

Bill lovingly watched his wife and her horse. She held Texas Lady by the mane and it seemed like they were one and he was happy he had given the horse to her. With her free hand, she waved at Bill once more. Just as Bill started to holler, "I love you," the lightning bolt streaked through the sky, illuminating the meadow in a blinding flash brighter than the inside of a flashbulb. The resounding concussion was so strong it knocked Bill to his knees and half unconscious. He staggered to his feet and ran, screaming, "No! no! god damn you, god damn you, no!"

His screams echoing unheard through the meadow.

Texas Lady lay as if life had never been in her body. A stream of blood oozed out of the flared nostrils. Her hooves had been blown off.

She lay several feet away. Her clothes and hair had been atomized, as if their existence had been a sin. Her skin was a bleached blue—the color of the sky on a pale misty day—blood trickled from her ears and nose. There were no gaping wounds but her body was only a shell.

Gypsy, the smell of seared flesh in the air, did not approach the bodies, but lay on the ground quivering and whining in prayer.

Sinking to the ground Bill held the blue hand tenderly and began rocking back and forth. "O God, O God, O God," he cried.

He barely remembered wrapping her body in a tarp and packing her on the horse like he would a deer. Her blood dripped from underneath the tarp and coated the side of the horse with her unfulfilled dreams. Riding off the mountain was a journey through limbo—a world devoid of life or color.

He did remember riding by a young man and a woman who were resting beside the trail. "He killed some poor defenseless animal," the woman said to the man, seeing the rolled up tarp and the blood, giving Bill a disgusted look. He did not acknowledge their presence.

The Woman
The Reluctant Spy

Sheila was almost skipping, not really thinking about the trees or the birds or even hearing the sound of her boots crunching the trail. Near the end of her journey, she found herself thinking about her life and her job. "You only like what people expect you to," she said. "You only own what everybody thinks you need. Simplify, simplify."

For the first time her house, her nice clothes, seemed only objects, something that had cost her time. Her life's time, wasted.

She daydreamed about moving to a small town near the mountains that would be bustling with tourists in the summer and rest like a hibernating bear in the winter. She would open a gift shop, sit in her shop and talk to people and look at the mountains. Wondering what she could put in her shop, through the trees she saw the edge of the meadow as if she was seeing it through a picture window. Stopping, she wanted to turn around, go back, back so far it would take her another day to return, another day to have not reached her goal, but, she knew it was useless. Taking two tentative steps she was about to enter the meadow when she spied the tent. She froze, like a deer sensing danger, and then stepped backwards, setting her feet down like she was tip-toeing into a sleeping child's room. She moved off the trail, hiding in the trees and gazed at the white wall tent with a mammoth stack of firewood next to it. "It's him," she whispered feeling elated but also like she was a spy.

A vision of the cowboy riding his horse swept through her mind. But, she could not see the cowboy. She wanted to go into the meadow and call out, but she did not, feeling as though a hand was squeezing her heart, making her chest tight and filling her with fear. Why she was afraid puzzled her?

When she saw him, sitting with his back against a tree, the hand holding her heart seemed to loosen, letting the blood return once more to her veins and washing away the fear. But, seeing his face, a deep sadness spread through her. Even from the distance she saw there was no hope in the face, as if the man was merely a shell, the cowboy boots and pants and shirt being held up by wires having no desire to be flesh and blood. When the man stood, she held her breath and retreated further into the trees, as if her presence would invade his lonely world and cause him to fade away into a dark void. But, even in her retreat, she wanted to run to him. She wanted to look deep into his eyes and hold him to her. She wanted to cling to him as he would cling to her and share his longing. But her desires could not force her feet to move forward.

The man started walking and she saw the dog. Even the dog seemed devoid of life, her head bent down, her tail hanging as if all spirit had been beaten out of her. Sheila held back a sob, a sob that stuck in her throat, a sob not really for the man, or the dog, or herself, but for a feeling that lay like a black shroud over the entire world.

Sheila saw a look of defiance start to form on the cowboy's face—the determination of a soldier, advancing toward the enemy, feeling he would die but believing, no matter how slim the chances, he would survive and his cause was just, but knowing the enemy also thought their cause was just.

When the cowboy disappeared from her view, Sheila inched forward until she could see him once again. All she could see was his back, a back that was strong and hard like the trees and rocks of the mountain.

The man stopped by a large boulder with a small pool of water at its base. Around the edges of the water grew red, blue, white and yellow wildflowers. The man removed his hat. He looked as if he were about to turn around, and Sheila stepped further back into the trees. After several indecisive moments the man put his hat back on and continued walking at a slower pace.

Sheila wondered what brought the man here, alone with his dog and horses. She thought about the men she knew, men who paraded around in bars and offices, needing others around them to define who they were, gathering around TV sets to watch football or baseball, cheering and shouting like noisy ducks at the antics of others. "I wouldn't invade your privacy," Sheila whispered. "I would leave you the trees and the mountains."

When the man reached the center of the meadow, he slowly knelt down, like kneeling before an altar, and reaching into the tall grass he pulled an animal skull from the earth. It was a large skull—a horse's skull she knew—the eye sockets like empty moons. He held the skull reverently like it was an ancient holy object. She did not see the tears that followed the creases in his face and fell on the white brittle skull. He set the skull down, stood up and gathered many bones and set them by the skull. When he could find no more bones he pulled up the tall grass until he had cleared a circle about ten feet around. He then picked up each bone and placed the bones in the circle like he was piecing together a puzzle, but she could not tell what the completed puzzle would be.

Stillness settled over the meadow, as if the wind had been sucked out of the world. Birds darting through the trees seemed to glide on silent wings and their fleeting songs were muted, as if, by choice, they would not violate the man's silence.

When the man finished, he stepped back, removed his hat and bowed his head. Sheila had a feeling she could hear his prayer, a prayer for peace and love, a prayer for solitude, a soulful prayer for the world, a prayer for himself, a prayer for the bones—all bones.

The cowboy put his hat back on and started toward his camp, walking quicker this time, like people leaving funerals, wanting to be away from the death, wanting to forget their own deaths for a few moments and go and eat cake and drink coffee and talk about living relatives.

Sheila could pick out small details of his face, a face that now looked peaceful with its crow's feet and sun darkened skin. His moustache made her think about cowboy bandits on TV. She saw the large knuckles on his hands and the way his fingers were swollen from work. Once again she wanted to call to him. She wanted to sit by his fire and drink coffee and when it was dark, she wanted to take off her clothes and dance for him. She wanted him to see her naked and feel his rough hands on her body, hands she knew would be tender. She wanted to mold to him like the leaves on a tree and give him her spirit—knowing in her giving, she would also receive.

She watched him as he started a fire and then patted the dog. The dog wagged its tail. He removed the dog's collar and with a pocketknife fiddled with something and put the collar back on. A few moments later, when the dog darted after some animal near the camp, she heard the tinkle of a bell like a distant church bell calling the believers.

Sheila took several steps toward the meadow but stopped, and turning slowly, walked down the trail. But, as she walked, she wanted to turn and run to the man. She wanted to tell him all about herself—tell him of her dreams and wishes.

Fifteen minutes later Sheila stopped in a dark stand of trees. She set up her camp and built a fire. "You are a coward," she told herself. "You are afraid to reach out even when your heart calls."

As the sun set, she was by the fire drinking tea and gazing into the golden flames. "I could have made you warm," she said. "I could have danced for you and made you smile."

Bill was sitting by his fire under a moon so bright he could see his shadow. Standing, he walked away from his camp and gazed at the muted dark treetops. There was a gray wisp of smoke hanging above the treetops that was not more than half a mile from his camp. He watched the smoke for a long time until he was satisfied it was a camper's fire and not the beginning of a forest fire and went back to his tent.

"I wonder if it's her?" he asked Gypsy. "The lady I didn't wave back to."

Gypsy wagged her tail.

He had the urge to saddle a horse and ride to the camp, but then said. "Hell, if it was her I would only scare her to death."

Gypsy wagged her tail once again. "You old worthless dog," he said.

Sheila poured the rest of her tea on the ground. "I'm going to see him," she said to the fire. "I'm going to his camp."

She ground out her fire and followed the starlit trail cutting through the trees like a gray ribbon. When she got to the edge of the meadow, she saw him sitting by the fire but instead of marching up to his camp, she stopped as if she had run into an invisible wall. Sitting, she broke a small, dry twig. To the dog, the snapping twig sounded like a gunshot, and Gypsy tore off into the darkness. Sheila's heart froze in her chest as she heard the dog's bell tinkling closer and closer to her. She wanted to run but knew running would be of no use. Gypsy, growling, inched toward Sheila. The dog almost upon her, Sheila was about to scream when the dog whimpered and poked her with her cold nose. Sheila rubbed the dog's face, almost crying in relief. "Gypsy," the man called.

Gypsy looked back toward the fire, waited until Sheila had patted her head several more times, and then ran back to the camp.

Sheila watched as the dog lay back down by the man's feet. "You chasing ghosts?" he said.

For over an hour she spied on the man, trying to force herself to go to his camp. But she did not. She could sense an invisible wall around him shutting out the rest of the world. A wall that cried out. "Do not touch me—do not come near."

He did not move often, only to toss another log on the fire or refill his coffee cup. He did not pat the dog. Sheila had the feeling she was watching man as a primitive and convinced herself that if she went to him she would only be intruding. She envisioned him as a man with his dog hunting food for his family or tribe. Man, maybe as he should have been, silent, alone, a hunter, one with a universe filled with hunters.

Sheila slipped away from the meadow. The full moon shone in the night sky like a gigantic lantern. She went into her tent, removed all her clothes and zipped herself inside her sleeping bag. "Tomorrow night I will dance for you," she said. "We will no longer be strangers. I will tear down your wall."

She fought not to cry as she tried to sleep—knowing there is nothing in life unless one reaches out and takes a chance.

The Mountain
Dare Not To Climb

A strange thing about mountains is that most people only see the tops. When a person stands and looks at the looming protrusions from the earth's surface, their gaze scans the slopes but comes to rest on the tops, as if the rest of the mountain is a mirage. A tired hiker, unable to reach the summit, will shake his head as if he were a failure, saying, "I didn't make the top."

People coming within a few thousand feet of the top of Mt. Everest, expending every ounce of their energy and mental fortitude, will not remember the great feat of getting there, but will only remember not making it to the top.

For most of the major mountains in the world, there are now helicopter services, charging a small fortune to take people close to the top. A person can camp and look out at the world and never have to waste their time with the slopes or the base of the mountain. People can touch the stars without the search or the pain. But maybe the base and the middle are what the search is really about?

At the base of the mountain is a town. At one time the town had over one thousand people. All that remains of the town are three lived-in houses, a gas station, a gun shop and a bar, all looking like hungry stray dogs.

It was deer season and Philip was on his way to the mountain in hopes of bagging a big deer. But first he stopped at the bar, which was filled with other boisterous hunters. There was only one seat left at the bar and Philip sat down by an old man who was drinking whiskey. The old man's face was wind-burned and cracked, his hands were like dried out boot leather and his hair was a bird's nest of white, gray and brown. His clothes had never seen the inside of a washing machine. But, his lips were creased in a grin and his eyes were those of a young man—bright and eager.

"Name's Ben," he said to Philip.

Philip and Ben drank and Philip learned the old man had been a ranch hand for years, making extra money at the time by guiding hunters—he had the reputation for guiding hunters to trophy animals. "Don't guide no more, too damn cold," Ben said, adding, "and besides I feel sorry for the critters now."

Ben had also been a hobo, a cook, an infantry soldier during World War II, a bartender, a dishwasher and had served a few years in the State Pen but he did not say for what.

As with most bars during hunting season, the conversation turned to hunting, each tale fortified with another drink. When last call was made, Philip looked around and Ben and he were the only two left in the bar besides the tired and bored looking bartender. "What's the hunting like on the top of Mt. Haley?" Philip asked Ben.

At the time Philip was searching for big deer and he thought Ben might help him.

"Ain't never been there," Ben said, draining his whiskey. "Ain't never bothered to go to the top of any mountain."

Ben then stood up and straightened his body—all of his bones slowly creaking into place like an old dog trying to shake off time. "I've never been to the top of any danged mountain," he repeated, his words slurred. "I've been every place else in those mountains but I never been to the tops."

He weaved toward the door. Philip knew in the morning he would not remember their hours of conversation. After several faltering steps, Ben stopped, turned slowly, and with a wry smile on his face and his eyes beaming said, "I always figured if I got to the top it was only downhill from there. Going downhill in life always seemed sour to me."

He turned back around and walked out the door.

Philip finished his drink. "He's been everywhere in these mountains," the bartender said.

"He's never been to the top," Philip said.

"Who gives a damn," the bartender said. "The top's the bottom to some, the bottom's the top to others, it all depends on which way you look at life, now drink up, I'm closed."

The Man
Embracing The Demons

It was eerie, for most of the night Bill had the sensation a ghost or being was hiding in the shadows and silently calling for him. Not calling out in anger or fear, but pleading. Several times he almost yelled out into the night, "Come on in, I know you're there."

It was several hours before dawn and thinking about the strange feeling now made Bill feel foolish. The fire was a glowing bed of coals, a last testament before its own death. Bill was sleepy, a sense of calm was radiating through his body, and for the first time in years he began to feel whole.

The two years since her death rolled through his mind like a slow wave of photographs. For the past two years he was only a bit player in his own life, not knowing his lines, or what he had said or done. The days and weeks and months of his life had gone by without his knowledge, the days returning in no specific order, as if Tuesday was Monday, or March was May.

Looking at the coals he began to feel warm, not warmth from the heat, but warm from a love that now did not hurt—love that could now be held, not as a crutch, but like a sea shell, or a pine cone, kept in a drawer as a memento of a special time.

Bill stirred the coals with a stick, sending a shower of sparks into the air, some falling back into the fire and others drifting off with the slight breeze to blink out before they entered the trees. Gypsy raised her head, put her head back down on her paws.

Bill stirred the coals one more time and thought about the bones. He had done what had to be done. "I should have come sooner," he said, making the dog raise her head once again.

He thought about the smoke from the campfire he had seen earlier in the evening. There was now no sign of smoke in the night sky. He wished there was smoke. "I could bring you coffee, or cook breakfast," he said. "I could show you the forest and tell you tales about the mountain."

He thought about the lady standing and waving at him. She was smiling as she waved and he ignored her, pushing her wave away, as if to say, "I wallow in my aloneness, I long for the dark."

He knew that when he did not wave back she had stopped smiling, wilting quickly like a wildflower, never seen, or admired. He wanted to walk into the trees and down the trail, she would be camped by the trail, afraid to venture far from the safety of other's footprints, and he knew he could find her. He would find her sleeping, a warm smile of forest sounds on her face. He would like to tell her he was sorry for not waving.

He did not remember falling asleep. He had not slept so deeply in years. There had been no dreams, no empty feelings darting through his brain as he fought for sleep. Gypsy was sitting watching him with her deep topaz eyes and jumped playfully when he moved. The embers were gone, now only a fine layer of white ash remained. He glanced at the sky. The sun was clearing the treetops and had almost burned away a thin veil of fog.

Bill immediately started packing his gear. Gypsy, always ready to move on, yipped and ran around in several small circles, making Bill laugh. The sound of his laughter was strange for an instant. Bill could not remember the last time he had really laughed and his laughter had been true, happy, not forced or sarcastic.

When the horses were packed, Bill poured water on the ashes and looked back at the trail he knew led to the camp of the woman. He mounted his horse and started for the trail, his heart racing slightly. As he came to where the trail entered the trees, he stopped the horses. Gypsy, who was already racing down the trail, stopped when she did not hear the soft thud of the horse's hooves. Looking back at him, she barked and ran a few more steps, stopped and looked back once again. Bill shook his head, "No girl, not yet," and he turned the horses.

Riding through the meadow he took a wide circle around the bones. The bones were how they should be.

When he got to the far side of the meadow where the trail entered the tree and started down a steep incline, he stopped. He knew he would not come back and he knew the meadow would not change. Not in his lifetime, nor many to come. Although the mountain was not a constant, it was a constant in his life. He burnt into his mind the varied shades of green from the trees and the grasses. He admired the boulders and the rolling lay of the land. He gazed at the jagged peaks beyond the meadow—the treeless ice and rock covered sides and everything seemed to fit, every color and contour as it should be. "It was a good place to die," he said softly.

He saw her smiling face in the rain as she led Texas Lady, her wave, and the childlike happiness that emanated from her, filling the distance between them with rays of love. Lastly, he looked at their old camp with the stash of decaying firewood and the circle of rocks for a fire. He noticed tiny white flowers growing in the fire pit. He nudged the horse. As he went into the timber he did not see Sheila enter the other side of the meadow with a smile on her face. He did not see her smile vanish or hear her say, "I will never reach out again."

The forest accepted Bill. He was not a stranger, he was part of the trees and the ground, the grass, the sky. He came to the mountains looking for himself after the war and came looking for himself after her death. The mountains were home to a god that most men did not seek—a silent god that spent eternity in the trees, revealing himself only occasionally to a fortunate few. "I think I'll start guiding again," he told the horse. "I won't do hunts, but I'll take people fishing, and people who want to take pictures. And when I bring people to the high country I'll tell them stories about the mountains and the people."

Bill could easily have made the ride back to his truck in one long day. There had been times when he had galloped off the mountain, turning the packhorses loose, knowing he would find them by the truck eating the hay he had left by the trailer.

When it was still early, he made camp. Not a hasty camp—he set his tent so the morning sun would filter through the front of his tent. He gathered wood slowly, savoring the breeze on his face and stopping to look at the varied wildflowers. It would be fall soon, the seasons were like fleeting dreams in the mountains.

That night as he sat by the fire and patted Gypsy he wondered. "Why was I afraid to go see the woman?"

Gypsy's tail thumped on the ground.

"You old worthless dog," Bill said. "What the hell do you know?"

Gypsy nudged Bill's hand with her cold nose wanting to be petted. "At least you let people know when you want to be touched," Bill said, picturing the woman waving and smiling and hearing, "hello, hello, hello," echoing down the canyon.

The Woman
The Touch Of The Bones

In the gray dark of early dawn Sheila made herself a cup of tea and listened to the forest stir to life.

Sheila tried to quell the excitement within her. Wondering if he would show any surprise when she walked into his camp or if he would be a man's man and remain stoic? She wished she had some lipstick, but then laughed, "That would be ridiculous, walking up to his camp with lipstick on. The painted hussy of the mountain."

Then she said with a frown. "He probably likes those little cowgirls with their tight round asses and cowboy shirts framing their boobs like wallpaper."

But, after a moment Sheila wished she had a pair of Levi's and cowboy boots.

She broke camp quickly, hoisted her pack onto her back and walked briskly up the trail. She heard the dog bark. The thought of turning around did not enter her mind. "I'll walk into his camp and I won't even ask him why he didn't wave at me."

About to enter the meadow, she put a broad smile on her face, held her chin up and slowed her walk so it would seem she ran into the cowboy by accident. When she entered the meadow the smile fell from her face like an autumn leaf falling to the cold ground. She stopped, feeling as let down as if she had been waiting in a cafe for a date who did not show.

She moved listlessly to where his camp had been. Her face was expressionless and her legs were like thick branches. She looked at the outline of where the tent had been and the spot where the dog had lay down for the night. His boot prints circled the fire pit. "You bastard," she said, chocking back a tear. "You heartless bastard."

She removed her pack and sat down, leaning her back against the tree where he had sat. She wondered what he thought about as he gazed into the fire and wondered if he thought about her? "That would be too much to ask," she decided. "Damn men," she cursed.

Sheila scanned the meadow. "We have at least shared this," she said, feeling the tranquility the meadow emitted.

She was drawn to the spot where the cowboy had held the bones and heading for the spot she felt like she was going toward something forbidden—a place for secrets that should never be told. She was invading something private and hesitated for an instant, but a magical force pulled her along. A force that was both powerful and gentle, like a male beast looking through blood crazed eyes at his baby and experiencing more than need for the first time in its life. Goose bumps came alive on Sheila's arms and legs, both chilling and exciting her.

When she got to where he had held the skull, she gasped, covering her mouth with her hands and took several steps backwards. But, she was not driven back by fear or repulsion, but as if she had run into an invisible spirit whose task was to guard the bones. Her hands fell to her sides like a puppet whose strings were released by the puppeteer, letting the puppet crumble to the ground, succumbing to his facade of life.

The bones were laid out in a circle about ten feet around. The leg bones were across from each other with the hip bone like a primitive war mask at the top—the vertebra were spaced between rib bones and other various bones to complete the circle. The skull was set on a flat rock in the middle of the circle so the eyes gazed toward the east and the rising sun. Wildflowers were placed on the skull—the colors stark and bold against the chalk white bone. Stuck in the ground, at the nose of the skull, was a wooden cross, about a foot high, made from two pine sticks lashed together with a leather thong. Hanging from either side of the cross, attached by leather strips, were two blue feathers that moved peacefully in the slight breeze.

The circle of bones mesmerized Sheila. She was not conscious of anything around her. She felt like her heart would fly from her chest and sail into the endless sky so filled with emotion it could never beat again, only fly. She could see the man picking up the bones and putting them down gently like fine china that would shatter into thousands of pieces with one wrong move. She could see him—grim-faced—his rough hands positioning the skull so it would always see the sunrise, the promise. She could see him plant the cross and tie on the bird feathers that were still filled with song. And then—she saw the man stand back and could feel the love he poured into the bones and the love he drank from the bones like spring water. And she knew the man had been lonely but had now learned to accept his aloneness. The bones had woven a blanket to keep away the loneliness.

Sheila knew more had died here than a horse, but, she also knew the site was a beginning, a washing away of the old and the embracing of the new.

Sheila moved mesmerized around the circle of bones. "I could have loved you," she said through barely parted lips. "I could have loved you. We have both lived with the bones."

She started searching the ground away from the circle. After a few minutes, she reached down and picked up a small vertebra that had to come from the tail of the horse. Holding the vertebra in the palm of her hand she understood its finality. She put the bone in her pocket and not looking back at the circle, went back to her pack, put it on, and returned to the same trail that had led her to the meadow.

Everything around her burned into her eyes and mind with a clarity she had never experienced. Everything was alive, the trees, the rocks, the moss, the dark gray of the trail. It had somehow bound her and the man—as if a cord of sharing held them together.

She marched quickly for over an hour but then slowed. She did not want to go back to her car. She did not want to go back to her world. She wanted to stay on the mountain and make her own world. She wanted to stand naked in the rain, hold her hands up in the air and scream out, "Why? Why? Why? Why do we burden ourselves so?"

An hour later she stopped in a stand of aspens where she had not camped on her way up the mountain. She pitched her tent and unrolled her sleeping bag. Later, sitting cross-legged and drinking a cup of tea, she removed the small bone from her pocket and set it on her knee. She could feel his strong hands running along the insides of her thighs. She imagined the stubble of his beard and his moustache rubbing against her breasts. She could feel her hips rise to meet his and the deep, burning, pulsating electricity of life as he entered her. "I could have loved you," she said picking up the bone.

When it was dark, she lay down on her sleeping bag, but she did not sleep. The bone, like a tiny ember, burned in her mind. "We have touched but we have not met," she said to the darkness. "We have shared beyond sharing but we have not met."

Rolling over on her side, she truly believed it was all her fault. Him not waving had nothing to do with it.

The Mountain
The Ravens

The Mountain
The Ravens

The eye sockets of the horse's skull cast away their shadows with the morning sun. A light breeze from the west fluttered the blue feathers hanging from the cross. High above the bones, two ravens rode the shifting up currents, moving their wings effortlessly as they glided in large uneven circles. Depending on how the sun hit them they were either a deep metallic blue or a glossy black.

The male raven, several inches larger than the female, squawked his raucous and echoing call, and moving his wing tips slightly, he dove to examine the fluttering objects far below him. His mate answered his call and followed his lead. They both squawked again as if sharing a joke no other creature could understand.

The two ravens circled above the ring of bones for several minutes, and with each circle, their calls became more excited. Satisfied there was no danger, the male raven set his wings and landed several yards from the circle of bones. Tilting his head he peered at the bones and the feathers before taking three jerky steps to the edge of the circle. His mate landed on the skull and peered into the left eye socket cavity, her beak poised like a spear fisherman. There was nothing to eat in the cavity and she hopped to the ground.

Both birds picked and probed at the bones for several minutes and then examined the feathers. Their curiosity satisfied, they took to the air once again. They circled the bones for several minutes, calling to each other before disappearing over the tops of the trees.

Within twenty minutes, they were back at the circle of bones. The male landed and set beside the skull, three-dime size quartz pebbles he had picked up from beside a stream. The female placed a small pinecone and a green juniper berry by the pebbles. All day they came and went, returning each time with some small treasure from the mountains: A stick covered with red moss. A yellow aspen leaf. A white piece of birch bark. A top from a sardine can. A red ribbon that had been used by a hunter to mark his trail back to his downed deer. Many pebbles of assorted colors and size.

Each time they returned, they took turns poking and moving their objects until they were satisfied with their work. On their last trip, they each brought a beak full of jay feathers and stuck them into the pile. Their creation was over a foot around.

They flew into the sky, circled the bones twice, squawked and then departed.

Over the next two days, two different types of people viewed the bones.

Unis and Richard were growing apart. After four years of marriage, they had reached a point where they both knew they either had to separate or try and work out their problems. They decided to get away from everything and headed for the mountains. After two days of hiking, they still had not found the magic that brought them together. They spent the days walking and forcing each other to talk about what they saw, but the excitement of one was only boredom to the other. At night, they sat on opposite sides of the fire, using the fire as a wall, but each wanting desperately to hurdle the wall, say the right thing, tell the other they loved them, but, the words did not come.

They discovered the meadow on the third day. It was Unis who saw the circle of bones first and it had such a dramatic effect on her that she called out, almost in fear, for Richard, who was on the other side of the meadow. Hearing her strained voice, he ran to her side. Coming up to her and seeing she was okay, he was so relived he hugged her spontaneously and kissed her cheek. Unis clung to him and pointed to the circle. "What is it?" Unis asked barely above a whisper.

"Indians must have done it," Richard said. "It's an altar or a grave."

Transfixed by the bones they realized they were holding each other. They smiled and kissed gently and holding hands they gazed at the bones and the feathers and the pile of shiny objects. "It's a circle of magic," Unis said.

They stepped into the middle of the circle and standing behind the skull they faced east. "It will see forever," Richard said. "It will see until it is dust."

Unis rested her head on his shoulder and shut her eyes. "We can make it Richard. I want to. I don't want to be like all the others."

"I know we can," he replied.

Still holding hands, they noticed each bone had been laid down carefully, so the curves were symmetric and the circle as unbroken as possible. "I wonder what the little pile is?" Unis asked pointing at the pile of pebbles, rocks, feathers and sticks.

"An offering," Richard said. "A blessing of the bones."

"We are nothing but bones," Unis said. "If we remember we are nothing but bones, we can make it."

Stepping out of the circle of bones, and still holding hands, they continued their journey.

The skull gazed east and the feathers moved silently with the breeze.

The next morning Mac rode into the meadow. He had been in the mountains for three days searching for strays. All but twenty of the boss's cattle had been accounted for and driven down to the lower meadows. He had been riding through dark timber, steep canyons, searching, but never finding the strays. He was growing impatient but knew he had to find the cattle or at least the carcasses. Riding through the meadow he saw the bones and stopped. He spit a large gob of chewing tobacco and wiped his chin. "Some freaks been up here doing drugs and screwing around," he told his horse and spit again, feeling angry.

He dismounted and picked up the skull. It was a good one, clean, and not yet old enough the bone had started to break down. He knew a man who would buy the skull for ten dollars. The man painted western scenes on skulls and sold them for up to one hundred dollars. Mac lashed the skull behind his saddle. "Damn freaks," he muttered as he kicked the pile of pebbles and sticks. He pulled up the cross with the feathers hanging from the cross arm and broke the sticks and crumpled the feathers.

Getting back on his horse, he spit once again and rode off to find the strays.

Late that afternoon, the two Ravens whirled around in the sky like two drunks coming home from a party and singing old college songs. When they circled high above the circle of bones they became silent and dove at the circle like angry hornets. They stood in the circle, gathered their scattered treasure and carefully placed it all back into a pile, adding the tattered feathers from the cross, and then took to the air once again. For several minutes, the two ravens silently circled above the bones before the male raven turned west. His mate followed. At the edge of the meadow the male called out, as if to say, "Damn people, they'll try and destroy anything they don't understand."

The Man
Turning Toward Destiny

Riding toward his truck Bill thought of his home, his few acres and the empty horse corral. He would sell his land and move somewhere where there were other mountains. He would buy some land where the mountains were almost in his backyard, not miles away, as distant as some unreachable dream or a dream not wanting to be reached. His living room window would face east into the rising sun and he would buy more horses.

Bill reached the footbridge that spanned the stream. It seemed several years had passed since he rode out. One person had ridden in— another out, both the same in many ways, but both different in ways that could not be touched. Bill's lips were relaxed and the scowl that had been part of his life was gone, her passing had become a truth in life, accepted, only the warmth remembered.

Bill looked at the sky stretching over him like a painted vibrant blue canvas. He looked at the dog, who was more than a dog. He saw a small flock of gray birds that turned in unison, as if controlled by one mind, and showed the brilliant blue of their underbellies as they turned. He stopped the horses by a small patch of red Indian Paintbrush growing beside the stream. The red was as vivid as fresh blood. He dismounted. Gypsy splashed across the stream, stopped, peered at him, and splashed back. Bill laughed.

Bill picked two of the Indian paintbrushes, rolled them up in his handkerchief and put them in his shirt pocket and led the horses through the stream and to the truck. The cold water felt good—a final baptism.

While unpacking his horses a station wagon drove by. A man and woman were in the front and three children in the back. The three kids gazed in wonder at Bill as they passed. Bill waved. The three children happily waved back. "Was he a cowboy, Mom?" a ten-year-old boy asked.

"I don't think there are any real cowboys left," his dad answered.

The boy was silent for a few minutes and then he whispered to his younger brother. "He was a real cowboy, I know he was. Dad's just jealous."

After Bill had the horses unpacked, he feed them and leaned back against the truck. "I wonder where you are now?" he said, thinking about the woman he had not waved to.

He could see her walking, enjoying her solitude. He could see her sitting by her camp, probably reading a book that named flowers and trees. He could see her brushing her teeth by a stream and hoped she had enough sense to boil any stream water before she drank it.

Gypsy lay by the tire, Bill sat down by her, put his hand on her back, and rubbed gently between her shoulder blades. Gypsy set her chin down on his knee and shut her eyes. Bill took off his hat and looked at the sweat lined band and the other splotches of dirt and grime. He never cleaned the hat. Each splotch was like a diary. He looked at his brown and gnarled hands and at the inexpensive gold band on his finger. It was difficult to pull the ring over his knuckle and when he got it off a band of untanned skin remained. Bill put the ring in his pocket—trying not to disturb the dog—but Gypsy raised her head and looked at him like a wife who was disturbed by her husband hogging the bed. "I wonder if she was married?" Bill asked Gypsy.

"If you would have ridden back you could have asked her," the dog's eyes seemed to say.

Bill took the bell off of Gypsy's collar and then loaded the horses into the stock trailer. It was noon and he could be close to home by sundown. He was excited, he would call a realtor in the morning and list the house. "How would you like to go to Montana?" he asked Gypsy, holding the door open for her to jump in.

Bill drove to where the gravel road met the pavement. To his left was the way he had come. The road exited the mountains quickly, went through a small town, and ran through the high desert back to his home. To his right, the road curled and climbed up and over the tops of the mountains, at one point reaching over 10,000 feet before starting its descent back to the plains. It would take several hours longer to get back to his house by taking the mountain road but Bill turned right and started up the steep grade.

Bill pulled over when he reached the top of the pass, checking the horses and making sure the trailer hitch was secure. Standing by the guardrail he could see for miles, mountain upon mountain. "You were good to me," he said almost in prayer to the mountains. "You were good to me and you were also bad. You've taught me a lot."

As Bill drove on he thought about Montana and he started to whistle.

The Woman
Fleeing The Dream

Sheila was walking so fast she was almost jogging. She did not see the trees, she did not see the sky, she only wanted to get off the mountain. "You bastard," she cursed, stopping and wiping the sweat from her face and then plopping to the ground like a wet rag.

"My whole life is a fantasy," she said angrily. "I came to the mountains to get away and I created another fantasy. Why did you have to ride by? You bastard."

Sheila continued her marathon pace toward her car. She wanted to get back to work. She wanted to immerse herself in so much work her days would once again become run-ons and she would fall into bed at night, tired and oblivious to life. She wanted to smile like a raccoon at her customers and tell them the house they were buying was the best in the world, knowing they were really saddling themselves with so much debt the house would become a burden. She wanted to get back into the myth of the American dream. She wanted to forget her dream about a gift shop by the mountains. "Who would want to do something that was enjoyable?" she smirked.

Reaching into her pocket she took out the horse bone and flipped it away like a troublesome pebble that had been in her shoe. She marched another twenty feet and stopped, sagging like a tired boxer. "I hate my life," she confessed and turned and went back to the spot where she had discarded the bone.

Picking up the bone gently she put it back in her pocket, feeling an unexplained sense of relief.

Sheila started her journey off the mountain once again, only she took her time. Her anger was gone, her resolve to get back to work and skin the public had vanished. Once again she wanted to find that small town and sit by the window of her store and look at the mountains. She wanted to go dancing on the weekends and hiking in the afternoons. She wanted a sign that read, 'Off To Live My Life', to put on her door. She wanted a closet with only a few dresses and comfortable shoes and she did not want to take twenty minutes in the morning to put on her face. "If they don't like my face it's too damn bad," she said.

When she was close to her car she slowed to a snail's pace, remembering for the first time in years what her grandmother had once told her, "Some people have goals in life, others simply want to follow their path in life and only live, enjoying the mystery."

"Only live. I wonder what it's like to only live?" she asked herself and then realized for the past few days she had 'only lived' and let her life go its own pace and path and everything was fine—the world had gone on without her.

"I am my own world," she said. "My only responsibility to mankind is to be caring."

The trail led her back to where she began.

"I am going back to my cage where all I will do is go from day to day chasing my tail and trying to find the door to get out," she said.

When she got to the car, she loaded her gear and sticking the keys into the ignition she was sad. The car started immediately. She rolled down the window as she turned toward the highway. "This poor world," she said as she reached the pavement. "Somehow we have lost our direction."

She knew, as she pulled onto the pavement, she was leaving her dreams behind.

Sheila was looking more at the valley than at the road when the left rear tire blew out as she entered a sharp right curve. The shock of the blowout caused her to over steer and the car screeched across the centerline. She was about to bounce off a guard rail when, more out of luck than out of her driving skill, the car darted back onto the right side of the rode and slid into a gravel pull off area built for large trucks to pull onto and let their brakes cool. Sheila was not hurt but she was badly shaken. Her hands were gripping the steering wheel so hard her knuckles were white. "Oh my God," she stammered, yanking open the door and jumping out like the car was on fire and about to explode. Feeling like her legs would fall out from under her, she staggered away from the car.

She visualized the car going off the guardrail and her dead body pinned in the wreckage. It took her several minutes to regain her composure before she opened the trunk to get the spare tire. There was a tire but there was no jack or tire iron.

She was afraid. Being stranded beside a highway was different than being alone in the mountains. There were thousands of weirdoes on the highways preying on women who traveled alone. She had heard the best thing to do if you broke down on the highway was to open the hood, get in the car, lock the doors, and wait for a policeman to come by. But, it could take days for a policeman to come by. The winding mountain road was not exactly a speeder's paradise and the closest town was over twenty miles away. She had a sinking feeling in her stomach.

Sheila opened the hood, got into the car and locked all the doors—forgetting to shut the trunk. "I should walk to town," she tried to convince herself.

"After all the walking I have been doing what is another twenty miles. Besides, it's all downhill," she said.

But, she could not muster the courage. The highway frightened her. She had enough food in her pack for several days, at least she would not go hungry or be cold as she waited.

A car with a man and woman came around the corner and she waved for help but the car did not slow down. "Get your butt out and walk to town," she ordered herself forcefully.

"Get going," she told herself again.

Sheila swallowed nervously and got out of the car. "No, it's not a good idea," she said and started to get back in the car when she heard a vehicle coming down the road but hidden by the curve.

"Stand here and wave for help, you sissy," she told herself.

But, as the noise from the vehicle drew closer, she got into the car and shut the door. She was looking in the rear view mirror when the front end of a pickup truck came around the corner. She looked away quickly and tried to sink lower into the seat, she did not want some half-drunk, woman-starved cowboy, stopping to help her.

Hearing the truck stop her heart started racing and she did not look out the window, feeling like a child trying to hide from the bogeyman that lived underneath her bed. She heard a man's boots hit the gravel and jumped, consumed with fear, when he knocked on the window. "You need help lady?" he asked.

She turned her head slowly, as if invisible hands were forcing her neck to move, expecting to see a man with fangs or at least a gun. "You need some help?" he asked again, squinting his eyes like he was confused, which Sheila, even in her fear, noticed were gray.

Sheila wanted to say, "Yes," but her vocal cords would not cooperate. She peered stupidly at the cowboy.

The cowboy stepped back from the window, took off his hat and wiped his forehead with his hand and then put the dirty hat back on. He looked at the open hood of the car and at the flat tire and went around and looked in the trunk. After what seemed an agonizing amount of time, he came back to the window. "Lady, I have a jack," he said. "If I scare you to death you stay in the car and I'll change your tire."

He did not wait for a reply and headed for his truck. In a few moments the car lurched from being jacked up.

"This is stupid," Sheila scolded herself, and with a sudden burst of resolve got out of the car.

He smiled a weather beaten, somewhat perplexed smile, still jacking up the car. "You look like a rabbit who almost got eaten by a hawk," he said.

She was about to tell him she had almost gone off the road and killed herself. She was about to tell him she was thankful that he stopped when the dog came around the corner of the car and playfully butted into her leg. "Gypsy," she said, patting the dog.

The cowboy glanced at her and then quickly turned his head, as though he was ashamed.

"You bastard," she said.

Straightening up, Bill took off his hat and held it in front of him. "I should have waved. I'm truly sorry," he said.

She was glad he did not say ma'am.

The Man And Woman
The Question

Bill put his hat back on. He wanted to tell her he had wanted to ride to her camp. He wanted to tell her he had thought about her, dreamed about her and even worried about her. Instead, he said, "It won't take me long to change your tire and you can get back on the road."

Sheila watched his back while he worked, feeling like she had melted and turned into a puddle that would sink into the earth. She did not know if she was angry or happy. On one hand, she wanted to tear into the cowboy. Tell him how his not waving had both ruined and inspired her first solo journey into the mountains. But, she also wanted to tell him how she had stayed awake at night envisioning him holding her, making love to her, and afterward, sitting by the fire telling her about the stars and the trees, explaining the sounds of the night. She wanted to tell him she had seen him with the bones and she had sat by the meadow and watched him gaze into the fire and, as she watched him, it was as though they were one—one with the dark, and the flames. But, she said, "You have a nice dog but you still are a bastard."

Hearing 'dog', Gypsy came over to her. Sheila laughed and patted the dog's head. Gypsy sat down by her, seemingly happy to sit and watch Bill work.

"She's okay," Bill replied. "And you are right. I am a bastard."

Bill broke the lug nuts free, feeling the lady's eyes on his back. A breeze swept up the canyon sending small swirls of dust from the gravel around them and causing the leaves in a stand of young aspens by the road to make a sound like a person wadding up wrapping paper after opening a birthday present.

Sheila knelt and put her arm around Gypsy. Gypsy made a deep contented noise in her throat and licked Sheila's chin, causing Sheila to say in mock disgust, "Yuck, dog kisses."

Gypsy licked her again.

Bill put the spare on the car. He spun the lug nuts on with his fingers and started tightening them with the lug wrench. "Why didn't you wave?" Sheila asked, with no anger in her voice.

Bill stopped tightening the lug nuts. "I was chasing demons," he said. "I was so far into myself I couldn't reach out."

"I was chasing demons by waving," Sheila said.

"Did you catch them?" Bill asked in a voice only slightly stronger than the breeze.

"I caught them and put them in a place where they won't harm me," Sheila said.

"They never go away completely," Bill said. "But they go far enough away they no longer throw a shadow."

Bill continued tightening the lug nuts and Sheila, seeing he was almost finished, did not want him to be finished. She did not want him to leave.

Bill put the flat tire in the trunk and closed the lid. "Well, you're ready to go," he said, shutting the hood.

"Do I owe you anything?" Sheila asked.

"A smile," Bill replied.

Sheila smiled and Bill noticed how sincere her smile was. He opened the car door for her and Sheila got in. She quickly rolled down the window. "Are you sure you don't want to be paid?"

Bill shook his head and Sheila could see a trace of sadness on his face like an old soldier tired of killing. "You keep those demons away," he told her and turned toward his truck with the dog at his heels.

In her rear view mirror Sheila saw him put the jack in the back of the truck and hold the door open to let the dog jump in.

Bill started the truck. Seeing Sheila watching him in her rear view mirror he waved. Sheila turned, smiled, and waved back. She started her car, turned and waved one more time, and reluctantly drove away.

"She seemed nice," he said to Gypsy.

Gypsy did not look at him but looked out the side window as if saying, "You idiot."

Bill pulled onto the highway.

A tear formed in the corner of Sheila's eye—a small tear that lay on her eyelid for several moments and then trickled down her cheek. She brushed the tear away. She pictured in her mind the cowboy riding across a meadow. He and his horses and his dog were antiques, something lost yet not lost, something going forward but looking back as if time would stop and take a deep breath and say, "We have gone too far, it's time to go back."

She turned on the radio, listened to an old sixties song for a few seconds and turned the radio off. The road leveled off and entered a wide valley. The valley stretched out like a green shag carpet. She fought the desire to turn the car around and go back to the mountain. Back to a world that was quiet and peaceful, back to a world that, compared to the world that waited for her, was as distant as a faint star.

Pulling the car over to the shoulder of the highway and leaving the engine running she got out. She could see cattle trails crisscrossing the valley like small dry rivers. Another tear formed in her eye—she brushed it away angrily. "You won't cry," she scolded herself. "You won't cry."

"I like that lady," Bill said to Gypsy.

Gypsy did not bother to turn and look at him as if looking at him would be a waste of time.

Bill felt sad and confused. It was as if the sun had come out after months of gray skies but then gone away in a few minutes—the hint of sun had done more harm than good. As he drove around a corner he saw her standing by her car and slowed down to stop, but he was suddenly afraid, afraid of reaching out, afraid of being hurt, afraid of trying. She smiled at him and waved. He smiled back and returned the wave as he sped by.

Seeing the truck approaching Sheila wanted to step out into the middle of the road and make him stop. She wanted to march up to his window and say, "Look, you dumb cowboy, here is my phone number, now you call me."

But she only waved and forced a smile.

"I could have loved you," she said watching Bill's truck and horse trailer go around the corner. "You could have loved me. We didn't span the distance without a reason."

After a few minutes Sheila got back in her car and drove on. Her face was blank, all emotion washed away like old makeup. "We are all such fools," she lamented. "Cowards and fools."

For over twenty minutes she sadly fantasized what could have been. Coming out of a sharp curve she screeched to a stop.

Bill was standing in the middle of the road. As he walked toward Sheila, her heart was fluttering like a young girl. She rolled down the window feeling both excitement and apprehension. Taking his handkerchief out of his pocket Bill unfolded it and handed her two small blood red flowers. "Indian paintbrush," he said, "one for your wave and one for your smile."

She did not know what to say.

"I think we should see each other," he said carefully, as if each word had to be chipped from granite.

A car pulled up behind Sheila's and honked. Sheila pulled her car over behind Bill's horse trailer and got out.

For over a minute they stood side by side looking into the distance but neither one of them speaking, though words rushed through their minds wanting to be said. Gypsy sat in the truck peering at them like they were children. Reaching into her pocket Sheila pulled out the small bone she had picked up in the meadow, holding it out for Bill to take. Bill took the bone and the bone spoke to both of them in an ageless voice. Holding the bone like a baby bird he smiled at her. "I don't need the bones anymore," he said.

"I don't either," Sheila replied.

Bill tossed the bone into some nearby scrub oak.

"Would you like to go camping?" he asked her.

"When?" she said, surprised.

"Now," he said.

"You mean now, now?"

"It's as good a time as any," Bill replied hoping he was not too abrupt and would frighten her.

Sheila hesitated, thinking of her work and her responsibilities.

"I know a small valley not far from here that has a lake filled with brook trout. It is only a short ride," he said. "I'm not going back to the mountain."

"I've never been on a horse," Sheila said.

"I'm a good teacher," Bill said.

"You don't even know my name," Sheila said.

Bill held out his hand and smiled timidly. "I'm Bill."

Sheila shook his hand and returned his smile. "I'm Sheila."

An hour later, after leaving Sheila's car in town, and buying a few supplies and a fishing pole, they were driving back toward the mountains. Gypsy lay between them with her head on Sheila's lap. Bill and Sheila were not talking.

There was time.

The Mountain
The Ravens Fly Away

The twenty steers slept on the edge of the meadow. Shortly after dawn Mac found them. After five days of searching he was overjoyed. But now he must get them headed down the mountain. If he could drive them onto the narrow trail at the end of the meadow, they would have to head down the mountain because the trail was so steep they could not dart off into the timber.

He inched slowly through the trees, not wanting to spook the cattle until he was in position to get them moving the way he wanted.

When he was above the cattle, he started shouting, galloping as fast as he could toward them. The cattle lumbered to their feet and crashed from the edge of the timber toward the middle of the meadow. The lead steer started to dart to the left but Mac anticipated his move and cut him off, sending the cattle back toward the middle of the meadow. The lead steer was the first to trample the circle of bones, sending the pelvic bone sailing into the air. The other cattle, close on his heels, scattered and smashed the rest of the bones, destroying the raven's pile of jewels.

When the lead steer saw the narrow opening for the trail, he darted for what he thought would be freedom. But once on the trail, he had to slow to a walk, the others following his lead. With the cattle headed down the mountain, Mac fell in behind them, checking if the skull was still lashed to the back of his saddle after the jostling ride. With the skull still in place, and knowing the boss would be happy he had found the strays, he felt good and began thinking about the cold beer he would be drinking later tonight. He also would call the man who would buy the skull and get his ten dollars.

Later in the afternoon two ravens sailed over the top of the meadow. The large male bird patiently scanning the meadow floor. After several minutes, he saw nothing to attract his attention and calling to his mate they veered away from the meadow. He did not remember the circle of bones. He did not remember the pile of magic.

It did not matter.